PROJECT: Mystery Bus

Other books in the growing Faithgirlz!™ series:

The Faithgirlz!™ Bible
NIV Faithgirlz!™ Backpack Bible
My Faithgirlz!™ Journal

Introducing a new Faithgirlz!™ series from Melody Carlson:

Girls of 622 Harbor View

Project: Girl Power (Book One)
Project: Rescue Chelsea (Book Three)
Project: Take Charge (Book Four)

Other books by Melody Carlson:

Diary of a Teenage Girl Series
TrueColors Series
Degrees Series
Piercing Proverbs
ByDesign Series Nonfiction

Check out www.faithgirlz.com

faiThGirLz!™

PROJECT: Mystery Bus

Melody Carlson

ZONDERkidz™

Project: Mystery Bus

Requests for information should be addressed to:
Zonderkidz, Grand Rapids, Michigan 49530

Library of Congress Cataloging-in-Publication Data
Carlson, Melody.
Project, mystery bus / by Melody Carlson.
p. cm. -- (Girls of 622 Harbor View ; bk. 2)
Summary: After cleaning up the mobile home park where they live, friends Emily, Morgan, Amy, and Carlie are given an abandoned 1970s bus by the park manager, who lets them fix it up and use it as a club house, and when they discover some old books, records, and journals hidden on the bus, the girls are intrigued.
ISBN-13: 978-0-310-71187-2 (softcover)
ISBN-10: 0-310-71187-8 (softcover)
[1. Clubs--Fiction. 2. Mobile home parks--Fiction. 3. Christian life--Fiction. 4. Oregon--Fiction.]
I. Title. II. Title: Mystery bus.
PZ7.C216637Pr 2007
[Fic]--dc22

2006021295

Editor: Barbara Scott
Art direction and design: Merit Alderink
Interior composition: Christine Orejuela-Winkelman

Printed in the United States of America

08 09 10 11 12 • 10 9 8 7 6 5 4 3 2

So we fix our eyes not on what is seen, but what is unseen.
For what is seen is temporary, but what is unseen is eternal.

— 2 Corinthians 4:18

chapter one

"I'm not sure which is worse," said Amy holding her nose. "That old musty smell before we started cleaning up in here or Carlie's Lysol. Pee-euw!"

"You want it clean, don't you?" said Carlie, waving her spray bottle of disinfectant in Amy's face.

"Clean, but not stinky."

"Look, this is the way my mom does it in our house," said Carlie, pushing a long, dark curl away from her face. "Are you saying our house is stinky?"

"I'm saying that — "

"Stop arguing!" yelled Morgan as she laced an orange and red striped curtain over a metal rod. "And instead of complaining about everything, Amy, why don't you just open a window and let some fresh air in here?"

"Wow," said Carlie, pausing from her scrubbing long enough to stare at the curtain in Morgan's hands. "That's really bright."

"So, are you the one complaining now?" asked Morgan as she held the curtain up to the window to see how it looked.

"I think it's pretty," said Emily. The fabric reminded her of a sunset. That's what she'd told Morgan when they picked it out of the big box of remnant fabrics. Morgan's grandma said they could use whatever they liked for the bus. "I thought I might make a crazy quilt someday," she'd told them. "But you girls could make that funny old bus into a crazy quilt too."

The girls' families had all been over to see the old bus on the first day that Mr. Greeley had presented it to them as a thank-you gift for cleaning up the trailer park. Mr. Greeley was the owner of the Harbor View Mobile-Home Court. At that time, the bus had been pretty messy with cobwebs and mouse droppings and dust and grime. The girls had been working hard since then, and the results were beginning to show.

"I wasn't complaining about the fabric," Carlie said defensively. "I just thought it was kinda bright is all. That a crime now or something?"

It was their third day of cleaning up the Rainbow Bus, and for some reason tempers seemed to be running a little warm this morning. Emily figured it could be due to the weather.

"Can you believe how hot it's getting already?" she said, hoping to change the subject. "My mom said it's supposed to get up to like ninety-six degrees this afternoon."

"I've lived in Boscoe Bay my whole life," said Amy. She pushed her straight, black bangs away from her forehead and flopped onto the narrow couch, "and I don't remember it ever getting this hot in June before."

"Another good reason to open some windows in here," snapped Morgan as she slid one down with a loud bang.

"Maybe we should all go jump in the Harbor," said Emily as she headed to the back of the bus where she'd been cutting fabric for Morgan. "To cool ourselves off that is." She sat down on the bed and picked up the scissors and started cutting out what would become another curtain. Morgan was teaching her how to sew and had even promised to show her how to use the sewing machine this week — after she mastered cutting, which wasn't as easy as Emily had expected.

"That's a great idea," Morgan called from the front of the bus where her sewing machine was set up on the small table. "We should go down to the beach today — get in this good weather while it's here."

"Yeah," agreed Amy. "Don't forget this is Oregon ... it could be raining by next week."

"We could take a picnic lunch down with us," suggested Morgan.

"Yeah, but let's get the rest of the junk cleared out of here first," said Carlie. "That will make finishing up the cleaning a whole lot easier."

"I thought we already cleared it all out," said Amy.

Emily glanced down the bus to see that Amy still hadn't budged from her comfy position on the couch. In fact that seemed to be her favorite spot. Emily shook her head and returned to measuring another eighteen-inch square — this one to be used for a pillow top. She didn't want to say anything, but she was starting to suspect that Amy Ngo was a little bit spoiled, not to mention slightly lazy. But Emily still felt like the new kid around here. Better to watch her mouth than to step on any toes.

"Yeah," said Carlie. "I thought so too, but then I looked under that bed and — "

"*Under* the bed?" Emily leaned over from her perch on the bed and peered under the bed at what appeared to be a solid wooden platform. "How can there be anything under here?" She knocked on the wood as if to prove her point.

"My dad showed it to me last night," explained Carlie, "while he was helping us to connect the electricity." The girls had gotten permission from Mr. Greeley to run a long outdoor extension cord from Carlie's house, which was only about thirty feet away. They couldn't use too much juice at a time, but it would provide enough to keep the little refrigerator running along with a light or Morgan's sewing machine.

"Here, I'll show you," Carlie said as she came to the back of the bus. "Hop off for a minute."

Emily slid off the bed and waited as Carlie bent over and hefted up the foot end of the bed. Once lifted, a spring mechanism attached beneath the plywood board caused the bed to fold into the wall. "See," said Carlie.

"Wow!" said Emily, peering down into what looked like a giant storage box. It was full of old-looking stuff. "Who knew?"

"Apparently my dad did. He said his parents used to have a motor home with the same kind of thing."

"It's so great that your dad's been helping us," said Emily, trying not to feel jealous of the fact that Carlie had such a cool dad. Emily's own father was an alcoholic who hit her mom — a lot. Emily, her brother, and their mom finally ran away with only the clothes on their backs to escape him. With a new last name, they hoped he wouldn't find them and take them back. So far so good.

"Yeah," said Carlie. He's going to take a look at the water system this weekend. He thinks we might even be able to use the sink and toilet."

"I want to see," said Amy, pushing past Emily to look under the bed.

"Me too," said Morgan.

Now all four girls crowded into the small bedroom area looking down into the random mix of boxes and things that were packed beneath it. So far the only things they'd removed from the bus had been rotten old curtains and nasty old bedding — things that had smelled musty or been chewed on by rodents. And right now that junk was bagged into garbage sacks, piled outside of the bus, and ready for the dumpster. But so far they hadn't seen anything like this. This stuff looked interesting.

"That looks like somebody's *personal* things," said Morgan.

Emily bent down and pulled out an old wooden apple crate filled with dusty vinyl record albums. "Jefferson Airplane?" she read the strange name on the cover and then flipped to another. "Bread? Who are these people anyway?"

"Weird," said Amy. "Do you suppose all this junk belongs to Mr. Greeley?"

"Hey, this isn't junk," said Morgan with real interest. She picked an album out of the crate and studied the back of it. "My mom had some of these vinyl records too. She almost gave them away, but I begged them from her. I've actually started collecting 33s for myself, and I happen to think they are totally cool."

"Want 'em?" asked Emily, holding the crate out to Morgan.

"Not so fast," said Amy. "What do you mean by 'collecting' them, Morgan? Are they valuable or something?"

Morgan shrugged. "Only to people who like them and collect them."

"Well, my sister An watches *The Antiques Road Show* all the time," said Amy. "And she keeps telling us that all kinds of junky looking things could be valuable."

"The most I've seen any of my albums going for, like on eBay, is only about ten to twenty bucks."

"Even so, maybe they should stay with the bus," said Amy. "I mean, since the bus belongs to all of us."

"I don't have a problem with that," said Morgan, slipping the album back into the crate. "But I don't know how we'll listen to them in here."

"What about this thing?" said Carlie, bending over to pick up what looked like some old-fashioned kind of music box. She held up the box and blew dust from the black plastic top causing Amy to sneeze.

"Bless you!" said Emily, stifling a giggle.

"It's a turntable!" exclaimed Morgan as she looked inside. "I wonder if it still works."

"I wonder what else is in here?" Emily stooped to pull out a cardboard box of books, both paperback and some older looking ones in hardback. She thumbed through the titles, noticing that there was a mix of mysteries, classics, and even some poetry collections — all which she happened to love. "Hey, these look pretty good." She glanced over to the built-in bookshelf over the back window. "Should I put them up there?"

"Take them outside and clean the dust off first," commanded Amy.

"Want me to use *Lysol*?" Emily teased as she carried the box toward the door. She didn't want to leave their unexpected treasure hunt, but it was getting stuffy and crowded in there. "Maybe we should take it all outside," she called over her shoulder, "to clean it off and get a better look."

So it was decided that they would empty out all the strange contents from the secret storage space beneath the bed. They hauled it outside to carefully examine each item, deciding upon its fate in the fresh air and sunshine. A lot of the things, like musty old clothes and mildewed tennis shoes, went straight into the trash, but other things, like the records and books, really did appear to be worth salvaging.

"It looks like these things belonged to a guy," said Amy as she gingerly dropped a dirty-looking baseball glove into the rapidly growing trash pile.

"Hey, don't throw that away," said Morgan, grabbing up the mitt as well as several other sports items that she suspected Amy had just tossed there. "These things might be collectable too. At least they look old."

"I can't imagine old sports junk will be worth anything," said Amy with an upturned nose. "Besides, we can't keep *all* this smelly stuff in the bus. We won't have enough room."

"Yeah, we will," said Morgan. "Under the bed, remember?"

"Yes, but why waste the space?" argued Amy. "We can use that to store other things."

"What other things?" asked Morgan.

"Hey, look at this," said Emily as she pulled what appeared to be a high school yearbook from the book box. "Boscoe Bay Cougars, 1979."

"Wow, that's a long time ago," said Morgan, peering over Emily's shoulder to see the cover of the faded red book. "Do you think it belonged to Mr. Greeley?"

"No way," said Amy, snatching the book from Emily. "Whoever owned this yearbook couldn't be much older than forty-five by now. And Mr. Greeley looks like he's about seventy. Maybe even older."

"The mental math whiz-kid strikes again," says Morgan, grabbing the yearbook from Amy and handing it back to Emily. "But I think she's right."

"Let's look at it," said Emily. She sat down on the sandy ground and flipped the cover open to expose a plain white page with several notes on it in various kinds of handwriting.

"Looks like this annual's been signed," said Amy.

"Maybe we can discover a clue as to whose this was." Emily sat down on the sandy soil and began to study the pages. The others joined her and soon they were reading the inscriptions out loud.

"'To Dan the man,'" read Morgan, "'Will miss you on the football field. Tight ends rule! Rick Byers.'"

"What's that supposed mean?" said Amy. "Tight ends rule?"

"It's a football position," explained Morgan.

"'Oh, Danny Boy ...'" read Emily. "'I wish I'd gotten to know you better ... Hang in there. Love, April.'" Emily laughed. "April with three hearts beneath her name!"

"She had it bad for Dan the man," laughed Amy.

"'Dan, Glad you seniors are leaving so the rest of us can have a chance at stardom too. 10–4, good buddy, Dave Cross.'" Morgan laughed.

"'You should smile more—,'" read Carlie, "'it increases your face value. Love and kisses, Kathy.'" They all laughed.

"Sounds like Dan the man was one hot guy," said Emily.

"Speaking of hot," said Morgan. "I'm cooking out here!"

"Me too," said Amy. "I thought we were going to take a picnic to the beach and go swimming."

"That's right!" said Carlie. "Let's hurry and get this stuff cleaned up and back on the bus."

"I know," said Morgan. "You guys finish putting this stuff back in the bus, and I'll go see what Grandma and I can throw together for a picnic lunch—that is unless anyone else has a better plan."

“That sounds awesome,” said Emily as she returned the yearbook to the box of books.

“Then we can run home and get our swimsuits and stuff and meet back here,” said Amy.

“I’ll swing by your house, Morgan,” offered Emily. “To help carry the picnic stuff.”

They quickly put things back in the bus and took off to their own houses to change. But Emily couldn’t quit thinking about this Dan guy as she pulled on the blue swimsuit that Morgan had given her when she found out Emily had only one outfit. Who was he anyway? And why was his yearbook in Mr. Greeley’s bus? Not that these questions really bugged her. No, not at all. Because Emily loved a mystery. And it looked like the girls had not only inherited a bus but a mystery as well!

chapter two

The Harbor water was shockingly cold at first, but the girls splashed in and out of the waves until they were thoroughly cooled off. Then they spread out their towels and blankets over the warm sand and opened the cooler that Emily and Morgan had carried down to the Rainbow Bus. At the bus, Carlie had insisted that she and Amy do their part by transporting it the rest of the way to the beach.

Emily didn't even feel guilty when Amy complained about how heavy the cooler was. She thought it was about time that the girl did her share. During their massive cleanup of the trailer park, Emily had just assumed that Amy was working as hard as the rest of them, but the more she thought about it, the more she remembered seeing Amy sitting in the shade or sipping on a soda or complaining about a broken fingernail.

"This is the life," said Morgan, lying back on her towel, a can of Sierra Mist balancing on her chest. The can matched perfectly with Morgan's lime green, one-piece suit.

"Yeah, I'm ready for some downtime," said Carlie as she straightened out her beach towel. "I mean, isn't this supposed to be summer *vacation*? And we've been working harder than ever the last couple of weeks."

"But our work has a good payoff," said Morgan. "Don'cha think?"

"I do," said Emily, stretching her pale arms out into the sun's warmth. Hopefully she'd start getting a tan before too long. She glanced at her three friends lounging around her on their towels and blankets. It wasn't going to be easy hanging with these girls all summer. Morgan's naturally brown skin glowed like copper in the sunlight. Carlie's deep olive complexion, as well as the way she was filling out her tankini, looked amazing, and even Amy with her relatively fair Asian skin looked a lot tanner than Emily.

Emily flopped back onto her towel and hoped that it hadn't been a mistake to come here without sunscreen.

"Better watch out, Emily," warned Amy as she reached in her beach bag. Then almost as if Amy had been reading her thoughts, she pulled out a tube of sunscreen and tossed it to her. "You need to protect your skin from the sun. My sister An made me put some on before I came down here. And it's waterproof too."

"Thanks," said Emily.

"Yeah, you could be a lobster in no time," said Amy as she adjusted the strap of her bathing suit top. Amy was the only one to wear a two-piece, but her figure was so much like that of an eight-year-old, it didn't seem too risqué.

"But I do want to get some tan," said Emily as she cautiously smeared some of the white glop onto her ghostly white legs.

"You could *use* a little bit of tan, girlfriend," teased Morgan. "You are one pale white chick."

"Thanks a lot." Emily tried to spread the gooey sunscreen even thinner now.

"I'll take some of that too," said Morgan when she was done. "If Amy doesn't mind."

"*You* use sunscreen?" Amy tipped back her oversized sunglasses and stared at Morgan.

Morgan nodded her head. "Yes, Amy dear." She spoke as if addressing a four-year-old. "People of color can burn in the sun too."

So, before long, all four girls had on sunscreen. And for some unexplainable reason this made Emily feel better. She lay back down, but instantly wished she'd brought along a book to read. Why hadn't she grabbed one of those paperback mysteries from the bus?

"Wanna make a sandcastle?" asked Morgan after the girls had lazed around for about half an hour or so.

"No way," said Amy. "Leave me alone — I'm almost asleep."

"Me too," said Carlie.

"I'm game," said Emily, relieved to get up since she was already bored, plus the sun was intense. "Although, as you already know, I'm not very creative."

"Maybe not when it comes to art," admitted Morgan as she went over to where some driftwood and things were strewn up against the sandbank. "But I've seen some of your poetry, remember? That was creative."

"Don't you want to build the castle closer to the water?" asked Emily.

"Sure. But we need some props and things to take down there."

"Oh." So Emily followed Morgan's lead by gathering up sticks and rocks and shell pieces until their hands were full, then they went down to the wet sand to select their building site.

Emily wasn't the least surprised when Morgan began drawing an outline and giving instructions for how to proceed. And, trusting Morgan's artistic sense, Emily just did as she was told.

After about an hour, their castle was nearly complete and Amy and Carlie came over to check it out.

"Wow," said Carlie. "That's awesome."

"Yeah," admitted Amy. "Not bad."

"Want to help?" asked Morgan.

"Sure," said Carlie. "How?"

And so Morgan gave them both assignments to gather more round little stones, some four-inch twigs, and any sort of seashell that they could find.

"Do you really need that stuff?" asked Emily. "Or were you just trying to get rid of them?"

Morgan laughed. "We haven't been friends that long, but you sure seem to know me pretty well."

Still, Morgan managed to put their items to good use when they returned about twenty minutes later.

"*Voila*!" she said, standing up and stretching her back. "Finished."

"It's a work of art," said Emily as she gave her a high five.

"Man, I wish I had a photo of it," said Morgan.

"I could run and get my camera," offered Carlie.

"Cool."

"You guys stay here and protect it," Carlie was already taking off. "I'll be back in ten minutes."

"And she will," said Morgan. "I've seen that girl run."

"You should enter the sandcastle-building contest next weekend," said Amy. "I remember reading about it in the newspaper last week."

"Oh, yeah," said Emily. "My mom was telling me about that. They're hosting the contest at the resort where she works. She said that people are coming from all over. It's the first one in Boscoe Bay, and they want it to become an annual event."

"Of course, there's a registration fee," said Amy.

"How much?" asked Morgan.

"I think it was $25."

Morgan frowned. "That seems stupid. Just to build a sandcastle when you can do it for free right here?"

"Yeah, but there are prizes," said Amy. "The first place winner gets $500."

"$500?" Morgan looked seriously interested now.

"And there are second- and third-place prizes too," said Amy. "I can't remember how much."

"There's Carlie," said Morgan, pointing to where the trail came onto the beach. "Right on time."

Carlie shot the sandcastle from a variety of angles. Then, as a middle-aged couple came walking down the beach, Amy approached them to ask if they'd take a photo of the four girls with the sculpture. The couple gladly agreed, complimenting the beauty of the sandcastle as the girls posed behind it for several shots.

"You girls are very talented," the man said, handing the camera back.

"Yes," said Amy. "We think we should enter the sandcastle-building contest at Boscoe Bay Resort."

He nodded. "I'm sure you'd have a good chance."

As the couple walked away, Amy turned to Morgan. "Why don't we?"

"*We?*" Morgan pushed her glasses up the bridge of her nose and frowned at Amy.

Amy nodded. "Yes, *we*. We could all chip in on the entry fee, and you could tell us what to do." She smirked at Morgan. "Which you seem to enjoy doing anyway. That would only be $6.25 apiece to enter the contest."

Morgan laughed. "You have it all figured out."

"And $125 apiece if we win first place," said Amy.

Suddenly all four girls were very interested. They all started talking at once. Some thought they should put their winnings into fixing up the bus. Some thought they should just split it and call it good. Then they talked about a compromise — half for the bus and half to split equally.

"Let's go back to the Rainbow Bus and start planning our strategy," said Morgan as she turned around and headed back to their sunbathing spot on the beach.

"Yes," agreed Amy, right on her heels. "And we'll need to fill out the entry form."

"And I'll have to start sketching some designs."

"I can provide the tools," said Carlie. "We have lots of shovels and rakes and stuff."

Emily thought about what she could contribute to the efforts but, as usual, she was coming up short.

"Okay," said Morgan. "I will agree to this only if Emily can be my right-hand man. I mean, girl."

"Why's that?" asked Amy in a somewhat insulted-sounding tone.

"Because Emily totally gets me," said Morgan. "And she's good at following directions."

"Hey, I don't have a problem with that," said Carlie in her usual agreeable way.

"Okay," agreed Amy with some reluctance. "I guess I'm okay with it."

So maybe Emily did have something to offer the group. At least she hoped so as she picked up one handle of the cooler. "Why don't you help me with this, Amy?" she said, waiting for Amy to protest.

"Okay," said Amy. "But only because Morgan provided the lunch and Carlie has her camera junk to carry."

And the four of them trekked down the trail and over the dunes and back to the Rainbow Bus, which was surprisingly cool when they got inside.

"Not bad," said Amy, immediately taking the couch.

"Siesta time," said Carlie, heading back to the bed.

"Room for two more?" grinned Morgan.

"Sure," said Carlie. "This is one big bed."

The three of them found their spots and within no time everyone was fast asleep, with Carlie even snoring. Well, everyone except Emily. For some reason she was wide awake. She just lay there for a while, thinking about the strangeness of her life these past few weeks.

Just the fact that she was here right now with her three new friends — sharing this cool clubhouse of an old bus, hanging out on the beach together, building sandcastles, planning to enter contests — was mind blowing in itself. But when she replayed the events of the past couple of weeks — dealing with bullies, fixing up the rundown trailer park, getting the hand-me-down clothes and colorful things for her room from Morgan — she couldn't believe her good fortune. And the most amazing thing ... inviting Jesus into her heart at church! Everything was so different from her old life — less than a month ago — back when everything looked totally bleak and hopeless. She closed her eyes and whispered a thank-you prayer, then rolled over on her stomach, hoping her mind would shut down for a while and let her sleep.

Then she spied the box of books down on the floor beside her. She was about to pull out one of those mysteries, but instead her hand paused on the spine of the faded, red yearbook. She still wondered about this Dan guy. Who was he and why was his high school yearbook hidden here? Was it just a coincidence or did he have something to do with this bus?

She pulled out the book and opened it up to the page with all the writing from his friends, glancing over it again, hoping to find some hidden clue as to who this guy was—who he might be now. He certainly seemed to be well liked. And, it occurred to her that he might even be missing this yearbook.

"Watcha doing?" whispered Morgan.

"Just looking at this," whispered Emily. She rolled onto her back, holding up the yearbook.

"Oh, yeah. Dan the man." Morgan sat up and leaned against the wall behind them. "Find anything new?"

"Not really . . ." She scooted up and sat beside her, continuing to whisper although it looked like Carlie was sound asleep. "I mean, we know that he's well liked . . . by both guys and girls. And he's good at sports."

"Let's look through the yearbook and see if we can find his photo."

"But we don't know his last name yet," pointed out Emily.

"Well, how many Dans can there be?" asked Morgan. "And we know he's a senior."

"Go to the senior section," said Amy.

Both Morgan and Emily looked up, surprised.

"And make room for me," commanded Amy, squeezing in next to Emily.

"Hey," said Carlie, nearly falling off the bed. "What's going on?"

"An earthquake," said Morgan. "Hang on for dear life."

"Wake up, sleepyhead," said Amy. "Nap time's over."

Carlie sat up and yawned. "What's going on?"

"We're looking for Dan the man," said Morgan.

"Huh?" Carlie blinked then looked over at the yearbook. "Oh."

They huddled together as they turned page after page, joking as they noticed some pretty weird hair and clothing styles.

"I have two words for these guys," said Carlie, finally waking up as she pointed to a guy named Carl, whose long, fluffy blond hair made him look like a girl. *"Hair cut."*

"I think that's one word," said Emily.

"Yeah, whatever," said Carlie. "Get out the scissors."

"Here's a Daniel Foster," said Morgan, pointing to a skinny guy with curly hair and wire-rimmed glasses. "Do you think that's him?"

"He looks kind of nerdy to me," said Emily.

"Not exactly the jock type," added Carlie.

"But everyone looks kind of strange in this yearbook," said Morgan. "It might be hard to tell what they're really like."

"Well, keep going," said Amy. "But stick your finger there."

So they flipped through the pages and were about to give up when Emily pointed to the bottom of the last page of pictures. *"Dan Watterson,"* she proclaimed. "I'll bet that's him. *Dan the man."*

"Even with his long hair, he's pretty good-looking," observed Amy.

"And he looks big too, like he could be athletic," said Morgan.

"There should be an index with more photos listed for him in the back of the yearbook," Amy said with authority.

"How do you know that?" asked Carlie.

"Because my brother and sisters have high school annuals, silly. I've looked at them before."

Sure enough, there was an index. And beneath Dan Watterson's name was a list of about a dozen more page numbers. They retraced their steps back through the yearbook finding shot after shot of Dan Watterson: football hero ... basketball star ... He even played baseball. And when he wasn't in a sports photo, he had a girl or two hanging on his arm.

"But I still don't get this," said Emily. "Why is this guy's yearbook in our bus?"

"Maybe it was his bus," suggested Amy.

"Dan the man?" said Emily. "Living in a funky old bus like this?" She shook her head. "It just doesn't add up."

"And why would Mr. Greeley have this bus?" said Carlie. "I mean, if it belonged to Dan Watterson?"

"It does seem a little weird," admitted Morgan.

"Maybe Dan is Mr. Greeley's son," suggested Emily.

"But his name is wrong," Amy pointed out.

Emily considered this. Sometimes names were wrong. For instance her own last name wasn't really Adams … but this was top secret. Other than Morgan, no one in Boscoe Bay knew her family's story.

"And here's what's been bugging me," said Carlie. "Why did Mr. Greeley have this bus here — I mean, for all this time?"

"We don't know how long it's been here," Morgan pointed out.

"Well, you saw the big heap of dead blackberry vines that Mr. Greeley removed," said Carlie.

"That's probably what he was doing while we were cleaning up the trailer court," said Amy. "Remember how he was gone all the time?"

"Anyway," continued Carlie, "that suggests that the bus has been around here a few years."

"That and all the dust," added Emily.

"Plus all the stuff that we found under the bed," said Carlie. "It reminds me of those boxes that people put stuff in and bury, you know … what are they called?"

"You mean a time capsule?" said Morgan.

"Yeah. Like a time capsule from ..." Carlie tapped her finger on the cover of the yearbook, "a time capsule from 1979!"

Emily nodded. "She's right. It does."

"Do you think the bus has been here that long?" asked Morgan.

No one answered.

"I wonder why ..." said Emily. "Why was it parked back here in the first place?"

"Maybe it was a friend of Mr. Greeley's," said Morgan.

"Then why did he leave it here?" persisted Emily.

"Maybe we'll never know," said Amy, hopping off of the bed. "But don't forget, we have things to do if we're going to enter the sandcastle-building contest. Remember, it's only a few days away."

"Let's put these boxes and things away first," said Morgan. "It's getting pretty crowded in here."

"I'll take care of it," offered Emily. "You go ahead and get your sketch pad out and — "

"See," said Morgan, patting Emily on the back. "That's why she's my right-hand girl."

"And I'll go see if can find that old newspaper," said Amy.

Carlie looked at her watch. "I have to go home now. I'm supposed to watch my brothers while Mom goes grocery shopping."

"Let's reconvene back here after dinner tonight," suggested Amy.

Morgan handed Emily the key, which was now hanging on a hand-beaded necklace created by Morgan. "You lock up, Em."

The girls agreed, and just like that the bus was evacuated — except for Emily who continued to carefully replace the boxes and things back beneath the bed. At least there was plenty of room now. And for the most part, the dust and grime had been cleaned. She was tempted to hang around and put the books up on the shelf. But she felt a little guilty for being in the bus by herself. The girls hadn't really made any rules yet, but this was supposed to be a clubhouse to be shared, not Emily's own private retreat. Even if she wished it could be.

She put the book box in last, standing before the still-opened bed as she tried to imagine what kind of a person this Dan Watterson really was and whether or not this bus had actually belonged to him. She'd noticed his name inside some of the other books and suspected that everything they'd discovered today had at one time belonged to Dan.

As she locked up the bus and slowly walked back to her house, she wondered something else too. If all that old keepsake kind of stuff really did belong to Dan Watterson — whoever he was — why didn't he want it back? And why had it all ended up in Mr. Greeley's possession? If she wasn't so intimidated by Mr. Greeley's grumpy personality, she might be tempted to ask. As it was, this might be a mystery she'd have to solve on her own.

chapter three

By the time they regrouped after dinner, Morgan had drawn several sketches for possible sandcastles. And everyone seemed to have a different opinion.

"I like the French one," said Carlie. "It reminds me of a fairy tale. I expect to see a dragon coming around the corner."

"But it's so expected," said Amy. "I'll bet half the sand-castles on the beach will look just like it. We need something special, something that will stand out."

"Why not the English castle," said Morgan. "I thought we could do all kinds of things with that open courtyard." She glanced at Carlie. "You could be in charge of landscaping."

"But it's so boxy looking," said Carlie.

Determined to not get into the middle of this, Emily was carefully reading the article about the contest from the news-paper that Amy had brought. "Hey," she said suddenly. "It says here that you can make *anything* — well, as long as it's not obscene. It's supposed to be 'family appropriate.'"

"Like I would design an *obscene* sandcastle!" Morgan rolled her eyes.

"But the thing is, it doesn't have to be a sand*castle*. Listen." And Emily proceeded to read how a winner from a similar contest had sculpted a ten-foot-long mermaid.

"A mermaid," said Carlie. "That'd be pretty."

"Someone's already done that, silly," said Amy.

"Good work, Em," said Morgan, pointing to the paper. "That's why she's my right-hand girl."

"Enough with the right-hand girl stuff already," said Amy.

"Yeah," said Carlie. "Like what are we? Chopped liver?"

They all laughed.

"Okay, let's get serious," said Morgan. "Everyone think really hard ... what would be cool as a sand sculpture?"

"How about a seahorse?" said Amy.

"Good, but too easy," said Morgan.

"A dragon?" suggested Carlie.

"Maybe ..." Morgan considered this.

"Maybe I should make a list," said Amy, snatching up her notebook. "Then we can vote."

"How about an angel?" said Carlie.

"Or a tyrannosaurus rex?" suggested Emily.

"How about a submarine?" said Morgan. "One that's just coming out of the water, but it's really on the beach."

"What about a pirate ship?" said Amy.

"How about SpongeBob SquarePants?" said Emily, and they all laughed.

"Slow down," said Amy. "I'm still on submarine."

"Hey, that's not a bad idea," said Morgan.

"The submarine?" said Carlie. "That was your idea, Morgan."

"No. SpongeBob SquarePants."

"I was just kidding," admitted Emily.

"But, seriously, it would be funny. And who else would do something like that?"

"And," Emily held up the newspaper, pointing to a line. "I just noticed here that you only have three hours to build it."

"Three hours?" echoed Morgan. "That would rule out pirate ships, dinosaurs, and submarines. They're way too complicated for three hours."

"But SpongeBob SquarePants isn't complicated."

"Go ahead and sketch it out for us," urged Amy. "Let's see what it would look like."

Morgan started sketching a square on two legs then laughed. "I'll have to watch cartoons to remember exactly how he looks. It's no good unless you get it right."

"But he's got those skinny little legs." Emily pointed to the sticks protruding from the pants. "How can he possibly stand up if he's made of sand?"

"Maybe he can be sitting down," suggested Carlie. "Like on a piece of driftwood?"

"Or maybe he's sunbathing with his little friends," said Morgan with excitement. "Remember, he has a crab and a snail and — "

"A starfish!" exclaimed Emily.

"That'll be perfect for the beach."

"Yeah," said Morgan "and they can have a picnic basket and suntan lotion and everything."

"It'll be so cool."

"And sure to win," said Amy. As Amy mentally divided up their winnings, Emily imagined seeing dollar signs in her eyes. "Let's fill out the application." She snatched the paper from Emily and started to fill in the blanks. "Uh-oh," she said suddenly.

"What?" they all asked.

"There's a deadline, you guys."

"When?"

"Tomorrow." She smiled. "Not a moment too soon, huh? Almost like destiny." She turned and looked at them. "Did you guys bring your money for the fee?"

To Emily's relief, they hadn't. But she suspected they'd have it together before she would. Maybe even by tonight. And while she knew that $6.25 wouldn't seem like anything more than chump change to most people, it was $6.25 more than she had at the moment. She knew she could ask her mom, but she also knew how tight things were right now. She'd been afraid to ask her mom for anything lately.

"Hey, maybe your mom could turn the application in for us, Emily," said Morgan. "Since she works there. That way we'd make the deadline for sure."

"Yeah, how about if we drop our money off by your house before your mom goes to work tomorrow?" suggested Amy.

"Sure," said Emily, trying to think of a quick way to earn $6.25 by morning. At least she wouldn't have to be humiliated by admitting to her friends that she was broke. At least not right now anyway. It was such a pain being poor!

It was getting late now and time to call it a day. "My mom and brother usually leave the house a little before nine to get to work on time," she told them. They all promised to drop off their part of the deposit before then.

"Here's the key," said Emily, handing the precious key back to Morgan as they stepped outside.

"I don't see why Morgan gets to have total control of the key," said Amy. "I mean, doesn't the bus belong to all of us equally?"

"Yeah, of course," said Morgan. "I'm just keeping it because Mr. Greeley gave it to me."

"But that's just it," continued Amy. "Why do *you* get to keep it all the time?"

"Why not?" asked Carlie.

"Because it's not fair," said Amy.

"Why not?" demanded Emily. "Morgan was the one who led us in the cleanup of Harbor View. She's the one who wasn't afraid to talk to Mr. Greeley. Why shouldn't she be in charge of the key?"

"Yeah," said Carlie.

"Because we should vote," said Amy.

"Vote?" echoed Morgan. "On what?"

"On who's really in charge here."

"In charge?" Morgan frowned at Amy. "Like someone should be the dictator? I thought we were all friends … and equals."

"Yes," said Amy quickly. "We are. But we're also a club. And a club has a president."

"You think we have to have a president?" said Carlie.

Amy nodded. "Yes. And I think we should have an election."

Emily sighed and Morgan groaned and Carlie just laughed.

"Come on you guys," Amy urged them. "If we're going to be a real club, we should take ourselves seriously. We need someone who's smart and able to make decisions to lead us. And I think I'd be perfect for the job."

They all laughed, except for Amy. Her eyes began to tear and her chin quivered.

"I'm sorry, Amy," said Morgan. "But I just don't see the—"

"I knew you wouldn't," she snapped. "You guys really don't like me, do you? I know it's probably because I'm the youngest one here. But I can't help it if I skipped a grade. I can't help it that I'm smarter than average. But does that mean I should be persecuted?"

"No," said Morgan. "Of course not."

"I don't mind if we have an election," said Carlie.

"Me neither," said Emily.

"In fact, we can do it right now if you want," said Morgan.

"No way," said Amy. "We need to nominate first. Then we campaign and make speeches and finally we vote—by secret ballot."

Morgan groaned again. "That's so much work."

"But it's the right way to do it," protested Amy. "And I'll bring paper and stuff. You guys just be ready to cooperate. Okay?"

With reluctance they all agreed. And as they walked back to their houses, Emily imagined that Amy was probably a natural leader after all. Except that she was sort of a dictator. Emily wasn't so sure they were ready for that. But why should she worry? Morgan would easily be elected three to one.

The girls told each other good night, and Emily unlocked her front door and went inside. As usual, Mom and Kyle wouldn't be home for a couple more hours. Emily was used to it now. And at least the place didn't look nearly as dismal and empty as it had when they first moved in. She looked around the house and realized that it had gotten pretty messy this past week. With Mom and Kyle working so many hours and Emily's recent projects with her friends, things had been neglected here.

Maybe that's how she could earn some quick cash. She kicked her idea into high gear as she went about cleaning up and straightening in the living room. She picked up soda cans, newspapers, and dirty socks. She dusted the few pieces of furniture that Morgan's mom had donated. She plumped the pillows. And finally — since they didn't have a vacuum cleaner yet — she actually got down on her hands and knees to pick up lint and crumbs from the dingy tan carpeting. After that she attacked the kitchen.

By the time Mom and Kyle got home, the place looked great. Well, as great as a somewhat rundown double-wide mobile home could look.

"Hey," said Mom as she came in the door and kicked off her shoes. "Someone cleaned up in here."

Emily smiled at her.

"What's the big occasion?" asked Kyle. "Are we having a party?"

Emily shrugged. "No. I just thought this place could use some help."

Her mom hugged her. "Thanks, sweetie. I appreciate it."

Emily wanted to hit her mom up for some cash now, but after hearing her gratitude, she wasn't so sure she wanted to spoil everything. She hated looking like she'd only done it for money ... even if it was the truth.

"I'm so tired," said Mom. "Such a long day. Do you guys mind if I just take a shower and call it a night?"

"Not at all," said Emily. This had been the norm since they'd moved here. "I've been busy today too and I'm tired."

"When are we going to get a TV?" asked Kyle as he poured a glass of milk.

"Hey, I almost forgot. Rita from the restaurant offered me an old TV that her mother-in-law gave her. She said it's in a cabinet that's as big as a house. I told her we have lots of room and that we'll pick it up this weekend."

"This weekend?" complained Kyle. "I'd be happy to go over and pick it up tonight."

"It's too late," said Mom.

"How about tomorrow?" he begged. "Please, Mom. I've been working hard and I'm so bored that I'm about to go nuts. You don't want me to start running around to find some excitement at night, do you?"

She shook her head. "No, of course not. And you have been working hard." She was starting to cry. "You've both been working hard. I'm so proud of you—"

"Yeah, yeah," said Kyle. "I wasn't looking for thanks. Just say I can pick up that TV. I mean, like ASAP."

"I'll talk with Rita tomorrow," she promised.

Before Emily went to bed, she read from the little New Testament that Morgan had given her. Then she prayed, finally asking God to help her to get $6.25 by morning.

chapter four

By 8:30 the next morning, all three girls had stopped by Emily's house to drop off their share of the entry fee. She thanked them and assured them that her mom would drop it off for them.

"What's all that about?" asked Mom as she rinsed out her coffee cup and set it in the sink.

"The sandcastle contest," said Emily, holding out the slightly rumpled application from the newspaper.

"Huh?" Mom glanced at it then looked surprised. "You mean the one at the resort? *This* weekend?"

Emily nodded. "Me and my friends want to enter."

"My friends and I," her mom corrected.

"You too?" teased Emily.

Mom smiled warmly and took the paper. "But there's a fee, Emily. $25."

"I know." Emily scooped out the bills and change that she'd been collecting in her pocket and set it on the counter. "We have most of it already."

"Most?"

"All except for my share."

"How much is that?"

"$6.25."

Mom nodded. "Well, how about if I cover you on that?"

"Really?"

"Sure. We're not totally penniless, Emily. And you've been doing such a great job of helping out. I'm so proud of the work you and your friends did for the trailer court. Hey, I'm happy to contribute."

"And we might win," said Emily hopefully. "Morgan is our designer, and she's really creative."

Mom smiled. "Yes, she definitely is. But I've heard that some very experienced sand sculptors are coming to town. And some people are really serious about this competition, honey. They practice all year long and go all over the country."

"But we'll still have a chance," said Emily with confidence. "Can you turn this in for us? Today is the deadline."

"No problem. I just happen to be going that way."

Emily put her arms around her mom. "Thanks, Mom."

Mom laughed. "No problem."

"I mean, for everything," said Emily. "For getting us here to Boscoe Bay and for working so hard. I think it's all totally worth it."

Mom nodded. "I do too. It's just been a little hard starting out with nothing."

"Ready to go?" called Kyle from the backdoor.

And then they were gone, just like every other day, and Emily had the house to herself. She straightened up the kitchen and wrote in her journal for a little while, but it was barely ten o'clock and she was already feeling bored. She wondered when Amy planned on holding their little election today. And since they still didn't have a phone connected, Emily decided the only way to find out was to go to Morgan's house. Of course, any excuse to go to Morgan's was a good excuse. She felt more at home at the Evans' than at her own home — mostly because there was always someone there. Plus, there was usually something good to eat.

"Come in, Em," called Morgan when Emily knocked on the screen door. Morgan was sitting on the living-room floor with a large tray of beads between her legs. "How's it going?" she asked, pushing her glasses up the bridge of her nose as she looked at Emily.

"Okay." Emily sat down beside her. "Whatcha doing?"

"Well, it was going to be a surprise ..."

"Oh. Want me to leave?"

"No. Why don't you stay and help me?"

Then Morgan showed her what she was doing. She had some alphabet beads along with some colored ones. "First you put on two purple beads, then two blue, two green, then yellow, orange, red, and finally magenta. See." She held up the leather string that was nearly half full of colorful beads.

"It looks like a rainbow," said Emily.

"Yeah." Now Morgan picked up a bead with the letter Y and slipped it on. This was followed by the letter A and N and another Y and finally L, which was really the beginning since Morgan had put the beads on backwards. Although it still didn't make sense. LYNAY."

"Who's Lynay?"

"It's a secret," said Morgan as she handed Emily a piece of string. "At least for now. So, can you make another one just like it?"

"Sure. Easy." And Emily followed the same pattern. Both girls worked quietly. Morgan showed Emily how to finish the pattern with another rainbow on the other side of the letters.

"That's pretty," said Emily. "But I'm curious about LYNAY."

The girls worked until they had four short strings of beads. "Finished," announced Morgan.

"What are they?"

Morgan wrapped one around Emily's wrist. "Bracelets."

"Cool."

"But it's a secret, okay?"

Emily nodded.

"Oh, yeah. Amy called and the big election is supposed to be at one o'clock today. Carlie had to babysit her brothers this morning. After the election, we're going down to the beach to practice our sand sculpture."

"Practice?"

"Yeah, we need to work on the size and who does what. Three hours isn't that long if we want it to look totally perfect. Want to see my drawing?"

"Sure."

Morgan pocketed the bracelets, picked up her beading tray, and led Emily to her bedroom where she produced a sketch pad with a detailed drawing of SpongeBob lying on a beach blanket with all of his little friends nearby.

"That is so cool," said Emily. "And it doesn't even look that complicated."

"But remember the sculpture is in 3-D."

"3-D?"

"You know, everything is carved and it has to have depth and dimension. It's not like we can just draw it on the beach and be done. I'm guessing that SpongeBob will be about two feet high."

Emily nodded. "Yeah, I can see how we might need to practice it."

"Want to take these over to the bus?" asked Morgan as she held up some pillows that she'd sewn. Emily recognized the fabric squares that she had cut out. "I finished some curtains too. We can make a lunch and take them all over to the bus."

"Sure."

They made a quick lunch to take with them. Then, loaded up with pillows and curtains, they walked over to the bus. As Morgan unlocked the door, Emily asked if she thought it was okay to be at the bus when all four girls weren't there.

"I don't see why not," said Morgan. "But I guess I don't know how the others will feel about it. I suppose it does make sense to have this stupid election so that we can sort of know what to expect."

"Well, we know that you'll be the one elected," said Emily. "I'm sure voting for you."

"That doesn't mean it's a shoo-in," said Morgan. "I mean, Carlie has a vote too. And Amy might make some really good points as to why she should be president. What if I voted for her?"

"You wouldn't!"

Morgan laughed. "Probably not. But I'd have to be fair. If I was convinced that she would be best and if you guys were too ... well, I'd have to vote for her."

Emily shuddered to think what their club would be like if Amy were president. She imagined a horrible dictatorship where they'd all work hard, and Amy would sit around and tell them what to do. It wasn't that she didn't like Amy, but maybe she didn't totally trust her.

"It looks pretty good in here," said Emily after they'd hung the new curtains and put the new pillows on the couch.

"Yeah," said Morgan. "But I'd still like to make something for the bed. That blanket on the mattress just isn't cutting it for me. And I think it needs a whole bunch more pillows."

Emily laughed. "Well, I'm sure by the time you're done it will be so cool that Better Buses and Gardens will want to feature it in their magazine."

"Hello in there," called Carlie as she and Amy came into the bus.

"How long have you guys been here?" asked Amy.

"Just long enough to hang some curtains," said Morgan.

"Looks nice." Carlie looked around and nodded.

"Campaigning are we?" asked Amy.

"Are we?" replied Morgan, pointing to the button pinned on Amy's shirt. "Go with Ngo?"

Amy laughed. "Just wanted to show you guys that I believe in myself." She set an empty tissue box, a small pad of paper, and some pencils on the table.

"Should we get this over with?" asked Morgan as she picked up a pencil.

"Not so fast," said Amy, snatching the pencil back. "We need to do nominations first."

"I nominate Morgan," said Emily.

"Wait," said Amy. "We need to take notes."

"Notes?" said Morgan. "What is this? School?"

"If we're a club, we should take notes," said Amy. "Actually, I mean minutes. We should take minutes. Do I hear any volunteers?"

Emily held out her hand to take the notebook from Amy. "Here, I'll do it. Let's just get this show on the road. We need to get out to the beach and work on SpongeBob. You should see Morgan's drawing. It's really—"

"Not right now," said Amy. "First things first." She pointed to the couch. "Everyone sit down." Then she pointed to the table. "Emily, you sit there so you can take notes."

"Yes, sir," said Emily.

"Don't you mean minutes?" said Carlie with a snicker.

"You guys!" said Amy, losing her patience.

"Okay, okay." Morgan held up her hands as if to surrender and then sat down on the couch. "Go ahead, Amy."

"All right." Amy continued to stand. "Let's begin nominations."

"I nominate Morgan," said Carlie.

"For what?" said Amy with a scowl.

"For president, of course," said Carlie impatiently. "I thought that's what the election was for."

"But we should have other offices too," said Amy.

"Other offices?" Morgan frowned at her. "What is this now? The military?"

Amy nodded over to Emily. "We need a secretary to keep minutes. And we should have a treasurer," she added.

"What for?" asked Emily.

"What if we win the sandcastle contest?" said Amy. "We'll need to keep track of that money and how it's spent. And we might want to start having club dues."

"Dues?" Morgan frowned. "Why do we have to complicate everything?"

"Fine," snapped Amy. "Let's just elect you as president and you can call all the shots, Morgan."

"No ..." Morgan shook her head. "Let's be fair."

"And let's get this over with," said Carlie.

"Okay," said Morgan. "I nominate Amy for president."

Amy smiled. "Thanks, Morgan."

"Okay," said Emily in an official-sounding voice. "We have two nominations for president. Do I hear a third?" No one said anything. "So, shall we consider nominations closed?"

"Yes," said Carlie.

"Hey, you're good at this, Emily," said Amy.

Emily smiled. "That's only because I was in student council back at my old school."

"Well, I nominate Emily for secretary," said Amy.

"Thank you," said Emily, writing down her own name. "Any other nominations?"

"I nominate Carlie," said Morgan.

"But what if I don't want to?" asked Carlie.

"Why not?" demanded Amy.

Carlie shrugged. "I don't like to write."

"You can decline the nomination," said Emily.

"Then I decline." Carlie grinned.

"Okay, then I nominate Carlie for treasurer," said Emily, feeling bad that Carlie hadn't been nominated yet.

Carlie frowned.

"You want to decline that too?" asked Emily.

She shrugged. "I guess not. But Amy is lots better in math than I am."

"But Amy is running for president," said Emily.

Morgan groaned. "And SpongeBob is waiting."

"Okay, okay." Emily looked down at the notebook. "Are nominations closed then?"

Everyone agreed that was enough, and so it was time for speeches. "You go first," Morgan said to Amy. "Since it looks like you're ready."

"Thank you," said Amy, standing up. "As you all know, I'm a little bit younger than you three. I won't be twelve until August. But you can't let my age or my size fool you. I skipped a grade because my IQ was extremely high and I was very far ahead of my class. As you know, I'm still ahead of our class. I've been the mental-math champion at our school for the past three years, and I've placed in district every year. I've won the last four spelling bees in our school as well as the last two years in district." Carlie yawned, and Amy frowned at her but continued. "I'm a gifted musician, playing flute, violin, and piano. I'm very self-disciplined, and I know a lot about business since my family owns a prominent restaurant downtown. I've lived in Harbor View Mobile-Home Court longer than any of you. I think you'll have to agree that I have all the qualifications to be president. I am a natural leader."

Emily looked down at her notebook and literally bit her tongue. Not hard though. Just enough to keep her from saying anything.

"Is that all?" asked Morgan.

"No," said Amy. "If I am elected president, I will take you all to dinner to celebrate — on me. Also, I will make sure that our club is run efficiently and in a way that will be appreciated by all." She made a little bow. "Thank you very much!"

Morgan started clapping and the other two followed.

"Next?" said Emily, looking at Morgan.

Morgan nodded without standing up. "Well, I think you guys know me. You know what I'm like and whether or not I'd make a good president. I encourage you to vote for whoever you think is right for the job. If you chose me, I'll do the best I can. But, as you know, I'm not perfect. Thanks."

"Is that all?" asked Emily. "You want to make a speech, Carlie?"

She shook her head.

"And I don't." Emily glanced at Amy. "Can we vote now?"

"Yes," said Amy as she handed out pencils and pieces of paper. "Cast your votes for president, secretary, and treasurer and then put them in the box."

"The Kleenex box?" teased Carlie.

Amy just made a face and began to write. Soon all ballots were cast into the Kleenex box.

"Why don't you read them, Emily," said Amy. "Since you are probably going to be secretary."

Emily opened up the papers and read them. No big surprises, but she hoped Amy's feelings wouldn't be hurt.

"Carlie has three votes for treasurer," she began. "And one is blank."

"I'll bet that was you." Morgan looked at Carlie.

"I have been chosen as secretary," said Emily. She looked at Morgan. "Unanimously."

Morgan clapped and the others did too.

"And for president," announced Emily, "three votes for Morgan and one for Amy, making Morgan Evans the first ever president of the Rainbow Bus. Congratulations, Morgan."

Amy frowned, but reached over and shook Morgan's hand. "I figured you'd win. Are you going to make a victory speech?"

"No," said Morgan. "But thanks, you guys." Then she reached in her pocket. "I have a little gift for everyone."

"Bribes?" said Amy with raised brows.

"Yeah, right," said Morgan. "After the votes were cast."

"Payoffs?" said Amy.

"Give it a rest, Amy," said Emily as she closed the notebook.

Morgan laughed. "They're not bribes or payoffs. They're just friendship bracelets. Emily helped me make them."

"Yeah," said Emily. "But I still don't know what they mean."

Morgan handed them out and the girls thanked her and tied them onto their wrists.

"They're pretty," said Carlie, "But what do the letters mean?"

"Who's Lynay?" asked Amy.

"It's an abbreviation for what I think should be the theme of our club," said Morgan. "And since I'm president, I'm going to recommend it. Of course, you guys can always refuse ..."

"What is it?" said Emily.

"LYNAY," said Morgan, "Stands for 'Love your neighbor as yourself.'"

"Oh," said Emily. "That's cool."

"I like it," said Carlie.

"Yeah," said Amy. "It's nice."

"The thing is ..." said Morgan seriously. "We need to love each other just like Jesus said to do. But we need to love each other just as well as we love ourselves — meaning we need to love ourselves too. Does that make sense?"

The girls agreed that it did.

"As your new president, I want to propose that to be the rule for our club," said Morgan.

"Just one rule?" Amy challenged. "You really think that's enough."

"I do," said Morgan.

"I don't know ..." Amy looked unconvinced.

"Well, let's see how it works for a while anyway," said Morgan. "And I was thinking that we should keep it kind of a secret rule. Like a secret code, you know. I mean, we want to live it in our lives, but we don't have to tell anyone what the letters mean. It could be just between us."

"Cool," said Emily.

"Okay," said Amy.

"Great," said Carlie, standing up. "And now let's hit the beach. I've got tools and buckets and stuff outside."

"SpongeBob SquarePants, here we come," yelled Morgan as the girls poured out of the bus and headed over the dunes.

chapter five

You guys ready for this?" asked Morgan on Saturday morning as the four girls loaded their tools and stuff into the back of Emily's mom's van.

"We had it down pretty well yesterday," Carlie reminded her.

"Yeah," said Emily. "If we do it like we worked it out, we should be fine. But we all need to remember not to hurry — that's when we make mistakes. And everyone has to do their job."

"And no complaining," said Morgan.

Emily knew this comment was directed to Amy. Yesterday, she continued to find fault with their sculpture, but it was mostly because things weren't finished yet. When it was all done, even Amy had liked it.

"If we can just do it as well as yesterday," said Carlie, "I'll bet we'll have a good chance at winning."

"We'll do it even better," said Morgan. "Yesterday was just practice."

"We'll win for sure," said Amy.

Emily didn't mention what her mom had told her, about how there were some very experienced sculptors coming today.

"Imagine $500," continued Amy in a dreamy voice. She nodded to Carlie now. "I hope that our new treasurer is ready to start calculating our winnings and the split and everything."

Carlie frowned and looked at Morgan. "Do I *really* have to be treasurer?"

"You really don't want to?"

Carlie firmly shook her head.

"I'll do it," Amy offered quickly.

"Do you want to appoint Amy to take your place?" asked Morgan.

"Can I?"

"Why don't we just vote," said Morgan. "Whoever wants Amy for treasurer, raise your hand." They all raised their hands. Morgan slapped Amy on the back. "Congratulations, Amy."

"But no speeches," warned Carlie.

"Are the sand sculptors ready to go?" asked Emily's mom as she and Kyle came out the door.

"You bet," said Morgan. "Thanks for going to work a little early today, Lisa."

"No problem," she said as she started the engine. "You want to be in time for registration ... and to make sure you get a choice piece of beach. Just yesterday I heard a couple saying that location is everything in a sand-sculpting competition." She laughed. "Although it all looks just like beach to me."

They were barely on the highway when they heard a loud bang and then a *thunkity-thunk* noise.

"Oh, no," said Kyle from the front passenger seat. "Sounds like a blowout, Mom."

Lisa pulled over on the shoulder and she and Kyle got out to see. Emily opened a window and looked out. "Is it flat?" she asked, worried that they were losing precious time now.

Her mom frowned. "Sorry, Em." She looked at Kyle. "You know how to fix a flat?"

"I guess I'm gonna learn."

"Tell the girls to get out of the van, Emily," said Mom. "On the passenger's side and stay off the road."

"We're going to be late," grumbled Amy as they climbed out of the van and went to the side of the road.

"There's nothing we can do about it," said Morgan, as she perched on the guardrail to watch.

"I'm sorry," said Emily as she sat next to Morgan.

"It's not your fault," said Carlie. "Besides, it doesn't take long to fix a flat. I was with my dad once and he had it changed within minutes."

Unfortunately, that wasn't the case today. It took Kyle and Emily's mom a long time to even figure out where the spare tire was. And then they had to figure out how to detach the spare and put the jack together. By the time they were done and everyone was back in the van, it was getting close to nine o'clock.

"The competition will be starting in ten minutes," announced Amy.

"We know," said Morgan.

"Do you think we'll be disqualified?" Emily asked her mom.

"I'll do everything I can to make sure you're not," said Mom as she drove down the highway. "But there's probably nothing we can do about the lost time."

It was a few minutes past nine when they arrived. Lisa hurried the girls to the registration area and they quickly got a number and an assigned spot on the beach.

"It's clear down at the south end of the competition," the man told them. "If you have a car, you might want to drive to save time."

"I'll drive you," said Lisa. "Kyle, go ahead and clock in. Tell Shelly that I'll be a few minutes late."

Then Lisa quickly drove the girls to the south end of the resort and pointed out where their spot should be. "Good luck," she called as they filed out of the van. "You sure you're okay for a ride home?"

"My sister An is picking us up," yelled Amy as they grabbed up their stuff and ran across the parking lot toward the beach.

"Look," said Morgan, breathlessly pointing to a sign just ahead. "There's number fifty-seven right there. We're number fifty-eight so this must be right."

"It's 9:13," announced Amy.

"We've only lost thirteen minutes," said Morgan brightly as she went for a big shovel. "No big deal."

"Just remember," said Emily as she took a flat shovel, "don't get too rushed. That's when we make mistakes. Just work consistently and listen to Morgan."

So the girls got to work. And it seemed that Morgan was right: Things were going better today than they had yesterday. And by 10:30 they all started to relax a little.

"It's not so bad down here," observed Emily as she neatly squared one of SpongeBob's corners. "We don't have a lot of foot traffic to distract us."

"Hopefully they'll come down eventually," said Amy as she worked on the crab. "I'd hate to do all this work for nothing."

"As long as the judges come," said Morgan, "that's what matters."

Carlie poured another bucket of sea water in their wet-sand area. Her job was to make sure they had just the right consistency to make the sculpture hold together. "I heard a guy talking when I was getting water," she told them. "He said there's this totally awesome sculpture of an elephant down by the restaurant."

"A standing elephant?" asked Morgan.

"Yeah. And he said there's going to be a monkey on top."

"Oh, dear," said Amy. "That doesn't sound good for us."

"It'll be fun to see it," said Morgan.

"Yeah," agreed Emily. "I can't wait to see what the others have done."

"You won't have to wait too long," warned Amy. "We have exactly seventeen minutes left."

Emily stepped back to look and smiled. Their sculpture might not beat an elephant with a monkey on top, but it was definitely good.

"Hey, that's pretty cool," called a guy's voice from behind her. She turned to see Jeff Sanders and Enrico Valdez from Derrick Smith's bunch of bullies walking up.

"Don't look now," Emily told Morgan and the others, "but trouble's heading this way."

Morgan looked up from where she was working on the snail and frowned. "Just what we need."

"You keep working," said Emily. "We'll handle this." She grabbed Carlie and walked over to stand between the guys and their sculpture.

"What do you guys want?" Emily asked the two boys.

"Hey, we're not here to make trouble," said Jeff, holding his hands up in the air as if to prove his innocence. He turned to his friend. "Right, Enrico?"

Enrico nodded innocently.

"So what are you here for then?" asked Carlie.

"We're just looking around," said Enrico.

"Yeah," said Jeff. "And it looks like you guys are making an awesome sculpture. Can we get a closer look?"

"I don't know," said Emily. "I'm not sure we can trust you guys."

"Yeah," admitted Jeff. "We can't really blame you for that."

"Really?" Emily studied the boys.

"We're done with Derrick," said Enrico. "He's definitely bad news."

"It's true," said Jeff. "Derrick's a moron."

"Why should we believe you?" asked Emily.

"Yeah," echoed Carlie. "How do we know you're not trying to trick us?" She glanced over her shoulder. "And right now you're wasting our precious time since we only have a few minutes to finish."

"Hey, sorry," said Jeff. "Don't let us keep you from finishing. It looks like you guys might actually have a chance to win something."

"Really?"

"Yeah, and to prove it, we'll get out of here. No hard feelings, okay?"

"Okay," said Emily tentatively.

The boys turned and headed back up the beach, and Emily and Carlie raced back to what they'd been doing before.

"That was weird," said Morgan. She looked up from applying some finishing touches to SpongeBob's face.

"Do you think they meant it?" asked Carlie. "That they're finished with Derrick?"

"I hope so," said Emily. She glanced up the beach. The boys were nearly out of sight.

Finally they heard the blow horn going off, their sign that the competition was over.

All four girls stepped away from the sculpture now and looked at their finished product.

"It looks pretty good," admitted Morgan with a grin.

"Better than pretty good," said Emily. "It's awesome."

"It's excellent," said Amy. "Maybe it won't beat that elephant, but it's definitely going to place second." She closed her eyes. "Let's see, $300 divided by four would be $75 apiece."

"As my grandma would say," said Morgan. "Don't count your chickens before they hatch, Amy."

"I'm going to take some photos of it," announced Carlie as she pulled her camera out of her beach bag. She proceeded to shoot it from several angles and even took a few shots with the girls hamming it up.

"Anybody hungry?" asked Emily as she opened the cooler and peeked inside. "Morgan's grandma put together quite a spread here."

"I'm starving," said Morgan, and all four girls attacked the cooler.

As they sat near their sculpture eating and resting, more and more spectators came their way, commenting on and praising their work. The girls thanked them, and their hopes began to get higher and higher.

"I want to go see the competition," said Morgan as she finished her last drink of soda. She stood and brushed sand from her behind. "Anyone else?" She started walking up the beach.

"I'm coming," yelled Emily.

"Me too," said Carlie.

"Don't leave me out," called Amy as she ran to catch up with them.

So they began what they agreed would be a quick walk up and down the beach to see what the other sculptors had created. And soon they began to see that competition was actually quite fierce.

"Wow," said Morgan when they were finally standing in front of the life-sized elephant who really did have a monkey on his back. "Not only is it huge, but it's got personality too."

"How did they do that?" asked Emily in amazement.

"Look," said Carlie, pointing off behind it. "They have ladders and everything."

"They'll get first place," said Amy sadly.

"We better get back to our sculpture," said Emily. "Before the judges do."

So the girls hurried back, noticing a group of what they were certain were judges only about six sites from theirs. But when they reached their site, they all froze and looked at it in horror.

"Where is SpongeBob SquarePants?" asked Amy in a small voice. They all stood by the sign for site fifty-eight. Their tools were there along with their cooler and beach stuff, but their sculpture had been completely demolished.

"Those boys!" yelled Emily. Carlie began screaming something in Spanish, shaking her fists as she did. Amy looked like she was about to cry. And Morgan collapsed onto her knees on the beach, bending over and pounding into the sand. "All our hard work!" she cried. "All for nothing!"

"What's going on here?" asked a woman's voice from behind them.

They all turned to see a group of six adults standing around their site holding clipboards and cameras and looking on with puzzled faces.

"We *had* a sculpture," began Emily in a shaky voice. "It was really awesome too." She pointed to Morgan who was still on her knees in the sand. "She designed it."

"But everyone helped," said Morgan, slowly standing. Emily could see tracks of tears down her friend's cheeks and it made Emily feel like she was about to cry too.

"It was really amazing," said Amy. "We thought it had a chance."

"But what happened?" asked a man in a Hawaiian shirt.

"We went up the beach to look around," explained Morgan. "Just for a few minutes ... and while we were gone someone totally destroyed it."

"Really?" the woman in the sundress looked skeptical.

"Really," said Carlie, running to get her beach bag. "I took photos just before we left." She pulled out her camera and held it up. "We have proof."

"Unfortunately, we can't judge proof," said a judge.

Morgan nodded. "Yeah. We understand."

"We're sorry," said a short bald man. "Maybe we can see about refunding your application fee."

The girls didn't say anything.

"Hey, what happened here?" said a man who was walking toward them with several others. "What happened to SpongeBob SquarePants?"

Morgan quickly explained their misfortune once again.

"Bummer," said the man, shaking his head. "I just brought my friends here to see it. It was really something."

"Yeah," said a woman. "Everyone on the beach is talking about it."

"You were the team who made SpongeBob SquarePants?" the man in the Hawaiian shirt asked.

"Yeah," said Emily. "That was us. We got here late and ended up with the last spot on the beach. But even coming from behind, we got it finished."

Before long about a dozen or more people came and began inquiring about the missing sand sculpture. The girls explained again and again what had happened, even telling about a certain group of bullies — without using names — that had messed with them before. And, while everyone was very sympathetic, it seemed there was nothing anyone could do. Even when Carlie offered to run and get her film developed, the judges explained that they had to see the sculpture for themselves.

"But we saw it," said a woman. "And it was really good."

Several others chimed in, but the judges said that it didn't matter. "Rules are rules," said the woman in the sundress. And slowly the crowd began to move back up the beach.

"It was nice getting their sympathy," said Emily.

"Yeah, but it would be nicer to get a prize," said Amy, and they all agreed with her.

"Well, maybe they'll refund our application fee like they said." But even as she said this, Emily knew it was a small consolation. Very small.

chapter six

The girls were just starting to gather up their sand-sculpting things when Morgan announced, "Hey, look who's coming our way!"

Emily glanced up the beach, shocked to see that Jeff and Enrico were actually walking directly toward them. All four girls stood in a line with their hands on their hips and grim expressions on their faces, as if they were prepared to face off against the pair.

"Returning to the scene of the crime?" Emily called out to the boys. She was definitely ready for a confrontation.

"Huh?" said Jeff with a bewildered expression that Emily, for one, was not buying.

"Coming back to rub it in?" asked Morgan.

"We just came to see how you girls did," said Enrico as they continued walking toward them.

"Yeah," said Jeff. "What did the judges have to say?"

"About your mess?" Morgan took a step toward the boys.

"What?" Jeff looked almost believably confused now.

So the girls stepped aside to reveal their ruined sculpture and both Jeff and Enrico looked truly shocked.

"What happened?" demanded Jeff.

"Who did this?" said Enrico.

"That's what we wanted to ask you," said Emily, staring hard at their faces.

Jeff shook his head. *"We did not do this."* He looked at all of them, directly into their eyes. "Honest. We *didn't.*"

Enrico held up his right hand like he was taking an oath of office. "I swear we didn't do this."

"Whoever did this is a total idiot," said Jeff, kicking the sand.

"Probably a red-headed idiot," added Enrico angrily.

"Hey, we did see Derrick Smith a little while ago," said Jeff suddenly. "He was on his bike, high-tailing it across the parking lot, heading *away* from the beach."

"I'll bet he did this," said Enrico. "Man, I'm so sick of that guy."

"You guys honestly didn't have anything to do with this?" demanded Morgan.

"I promise you, we didn't," said Jeff. "Like I said earlier, we've had it with Derrick. He's certifiable. We don't need his kind of trouble."

"Did you guys see Derrick at all?" asked Enrico suddenly.

The girls admitted that they hadn't. "But we did see you guys," Emily reminded the boys, still not totally convinced of their innocence.

"Do you really think we'd come back like this if we'd done that?" asked Jeff.

Morgan shrugged.

"Well, you should believe us. We didn't do it. But we'll be on the lookout for Derrick now," said Enrico. "If we find him, we'll find out whether or not he was involved."

"A lot of good that will do us now," said Carlie as she stooped to pick up a hoe.

"Hey, you want us to beat him up for you?" asked Enrico, making a fist for her.

This actually made Carlie laugh.

"No, that's not necessary," Morgan said quickly. "As much as I'd like to hurt someone, we don't need any more violence."

"But thanks for the offer," said Emily sarcastically.

"Well, if it makes you feel any better," added Jeff, "we're sorry this happened to you girls. We thought your sculpture had a really good chance of winning a prize."

"Thanks," said Morgan. The other girls thanked them too, and then the boys left. They finished gathering up their stuff and started getting ready to leave since it was pointless to stick around. Amy had already called her sister An and told her the bad news and asked her to come get them early.

"She should be here any minute," said Amy as she began trekking away from the beach with a shovel and a bucket in hand.

The girls stood on the edge of the parking lot, waiting quietly for An. It seemed clear that they were all tired — not to mention discouraged. No one wanted to talk. After about five minutes An showed up, and they quickly loaded their stuff into the back of her Honda. No one said anything as she drove back toward town.

"Sorry about your ruined day," An said as she stopped at the red light. "Amy told me the whole sad story."

"Yeah, what a disaster," said Carlie.

"Not completely," said Morgan. "At least we made some friends today."

"Who?" An glanced curiously at Morgan.

"Well, for one thing, it was amazing how the other sculptors were really sympathetic toward us and even told us that they thought we might've had a chance to win."

"Yeah," agreed Emily. "That was pretty cool."

"And I have pictures in my camera," added Carlie. "So we can always prove how good our sculpture really was, once I get them developed that is."

"And then there was that last thing ..." Morgan continued talking to An. "With these two guys, Enrico and Jeff ... They're like a year older than us and usually just act like big, stupid bullies. But today they weren't so bad."

"And it was a relief to find out that they weren't involved," added Emily.

"At least we *think* they weren't," said Carlie.

"They were actually really nice to us," said Amy.

An laughed. "Well, they should be nice. You're cute, sweet girls, and if those boys have any sense they'll figure that out before long."

An dropped them at Harbor View, and they all gathered their things and trudged off to their own houses without saying much. Emily suspected that everyone was just as tired and discouraged as she felt. And while it was somewhat encouraging to hear Morgan's optimistic take on the whole thing, Emily still felt pretty depressed about it. It just seemed so unfair. So wrong.

But that wasn't the only thing bugging her as she came inside, locked the door, and dumped her stuff on the floor. She also felt partially to blame for the whole stupid thing. If she hadn't offered for her mom to drive them to the resort on her way to work, they might've gone with someone else, someone who wouldn't have gotten a flat tire, and consequently they would have gotten there on time. And if they'd gotten there on time, they could've gotten a better site. And, instead of being off on the end where people didn't notice what was going on, they could've been right in the center of things where no one would've been able to destroy their entry. Naturally none of her friends had mentioned this, but Emily knew it was true. And she suspected that they knew it too. They were probably all blaming her right now. She was a mess-up and a loser. Worse than that, she was probably a jinx. She remembered how her dad once told her she was a jinx — and that she brought bad luck to people. Maybe it was true.

She took a long shower and then — exhausted from the events of the day and wanting to stop thinking about how the whole thing was all her fault — she decided to take a nap. As usual, her air mattress was partially deflated, but she didn't even care. She figured it was what she deserved. And it didn't keep her from falling fast asleep.

But when she woke up, it was with a start! Someone was pounding on her bedroom window, trying to break in. Worried that it was a burglar or an ax murderer or her dad, she ran into the bathroom and locked herself in. Okay, maybe it wasn't the smartest thing to do, but since they still had no phone in the house, it was better than nothing. She held her breath and listened intently, wondering if the intruder was still trying to get in.

"*Emily!*" She heard Morgan's voice yelling at her from somewhere outside. "*Are you in there? Answer me!*"

Emily quickly ran out of the bathroom to unlock the front door. "I'm over here, Morgan!" she yelled, still frightened that she might be in danger. "In front of my house!"

"Oh, there you are," said Morgan as she ran up the steps where Emily was standing. "I really wish you guys would get a phone!"

"Next week," said Emily. "Mom promised. Was that you beating on my window?"

"Yeah." Morgan leaned against the porch railing to catch her breath. "No one answered the door."

"So what's going on?" asked Emily. "Why are you running around the neighborhood and scaring people half to death?"

"I'm calling an emergency club meeting," said Morgan. "Be there in ten minutes — or else!" Then, just like that, she ran off toward her own house.

Wondering what on earth was going on, Emily went back inside, put on a sweatshirt, and quickly ran a brush through her hair. She wrote her mom a note and then headed over to the Rainbow Bus. Naturally, she was the first one there, so she sat down on the bus's steps and tried to figure out why Morgan would call an emergency meeting. Maybe they had to talk about how to handle Derrick Smith. Perhaps Morgan had decided not to let him get away with his latest attack of meanness. Maybe she planned to call the police and press charges. Of course, they didn't know for sure that it was Derrick this time, even though it did seem to have his fingerprints all over it.

"Hey, you," called Morgan as she hurried up toward the bus. She had a bag in one hand and the key to the bus in the other.

"Want some help?" asked Emily.

Morgan handed her the bag as she unlocked and opened the door.

"So, what's up?" asked Emily as they went inside.

"We have to wait for the others," said Morgan as she opened a window to let in some fresh air.

"I thought I was your right-hand girl," said Emily.

Morgan nodded. "You are. But I just want to be fair. Okay?"

Emily sank down onto the couch, folding her arms across her chest as if she were offended, but then said, "Okay."

Carlie and Amy ran up and bounded into the bus.

"What's going on?" demanded Carlie. "My dad said you called and said it was an emergency." She sat down at the dining table and looked at Morgan.

"Yeah," said Amy. "What gives, Morgan? I'm supposed to help at the restaurant tonight and I can only stay a few minutes."

"Yeah," said Carlie. "I need to get back too. I'm supposed to set the table. Besides I'm starving."

"Here," said Morgan opening the brown bag and taking out four large brownies and handing them around. "Hope this doesn't spoil your dinner."

"No way," said Carlie, taking one. "I could eat all four of those and still be hungry for supper. Man, we worked so hard today. I'll bet we burned off thousands of calories."

"That's right," said Morgan with a huge smile. "We did work hard. In fact, that's exactly why I called this emergency meeting. You see, I just got a phone call ..."

"Yeah?" said Emily, leaning forward.

"From the Boscoe Bay Resort ..." Morgan continued in a mysterious voice. "Apparently, Emily's mom gave them my name and phone number."

"But why?" demanded Amy.

"Come on," said Carlie. "What gives?"

"Well, it's about the sand-sculpting contest," Morgan continued. "It seems that the committee decided to have what they call a 'People's Choice Award.'"

"What's that?" asked Carlie.

"They put out a ballot box, right there on the beach," she winked at Amy, "and probably not a Kleenex box either. And they invited everyone, including contestants and spectators, to write in the number of their favorite sand-sculpture entry. And ..." Morgan paused.

"And?" Emily was pulling on Morgan's arm, trying to get her to quit stringing them along.

"And we won." Morgan calmly smiled at the others.

"We won?" said Amy.

"Yeah!" Morgan yelled the good news now. *"We won!"* And then all four girls were laughing and jumping and hugging each other, so much that the bus was actually rocking with their movements. Finally they quieted down.

"So, what did we win?" asked Carlie.

"Well, along with the ballot box, it seems they also put out another box that was for donations. The People's Choice Award gets a prize that's totally donated, and the amount given was $378."

"$378?" Emily echoed in amazement.

"That's $94.50 each," said Amy without even blinking.

"Or something like that," said Morgan, rolling her eyes.

"No, that's correct." said Amy seriously, "you can check it on a calculator." The other girls laughed.

"How much is it if we put half of the total back into the bus?" asked Emily.

Amy paused for about a second and then said, "That would be $47.25 each, and then we'd have $189 to use for the bus."

"How does she do that?" Carlie scratched her head with a puzzled expression.

"It's a gift," said Morgan.

"I can't believe it," said Emily. "We really won the People's Choice Award?"

"It's true," said Morgan. "Oh, yeah, Carlie, the manager at the resort asked if you could get those pictures developed in time to go in Tuesday's newspaper?"

"Wow, we're going to be in the newspaper again?" said Amy. "That's twice in one month!"

"It's a small town," said Morgan.

Emily just hoped it was small enough that her dad wouldn't somehow get wind of this. Of course, she reminded herself, her dad seldom read the newspaper or watched the news. He thought it was all "a bunch of propaganda."

"No problem," said Carlie. "I'll ask dad to drop my film off at the overnight place tonight. We can have prints by tomorrow."

"This is so great," said Amy, "But I better get back before my brother decides to leave for the restaurant without me."

"Group hug first," said Morgan. And all three girls embraced for a good, tight group hug. Then she held up her arm with the rainbow bracelet on it. "Way to go, girls," she said. The others held up their bracelets too.

"Rainbows rule!" said Amy.

"Rainbows rule!" echoed the others.

"Let's meet tomorrow afternoon," said Morgan as they went out and waited for her to lock up the bus. "After church. Like two o'clock?"

"Sounds good to me," said Amy.

"Maybe my photos will be done by then," said Carlie.

Then they all said good-bye, heading their separate ways. And, as Emily went into her house, she felt a renewed sense of hope. Maybe she hadn't jinxed the group after all. Maybe with God in her life, things really were changing.

chapter seven

On Sunday, the girls met at two. They decided to walk to town to see if Carlie's prints were ready yet. Fortunately they were, and after carefully looking at all of them, they picked out several that looked really good. They walked over to the newspaper office only to find that it was closed.

"We'll bring them first thing tomorrow," said Morgan.

Back at the Rainbow Bus, the girls settled in, opened some windows for fresh air, and shared a bag of Oreos provided by Carlie.

"When do we get the prize money?" asked Amy.

"The guy at the hotel said we can pick it up on Monday. He wants us all to come so we can get our picture taken."

"Maybe we can just give him one of these," said Carlie, holding up the packet of photos.

"My mom could give us a ride to the resort," said Emily. "But then she couldn't bring us home."

"And it's a long walk," said Carlie.

"I'll ask Grandma to drive us," said Morgan.

"Should we decide how we want to use our prize money for the bus?" asked Amy, setting the notebook on the table like she was ready to start writing things down.

"I thought I was the secretary," said Emily, sliding the notebook over to herself.

"Is this an official meeting?" asked Morgan.

"I don't know, Madam President," said Amy. "Is it?"

Morgan shrugged. "Why not?"

"Are you going to call the meeting to order?" asked Amy.

"Okay," said Morgan in an even voice. "I realize that you like to do things your way, Amy, but since I'm president, I get to run the meeting my way. And I'm not into all that fancy-schmancy meeting rules stuff. I mean, it's fine for Emily to take notes, if she wants to and needs to, and you can do whatever you think a treasurer should do. But I am a free spirit and I refuse to be put in a box."

"Amen!" said Emily, stifling a giggle.

Morgan laughed. "You sound just like Walter Alpenheimer."

"Who's Walter Alpenheimer?" asked Amy.

"This guy at church who always says 'Amen' after everything."

"Amen," said Emily again.

"So, am I clear?" asked Morgan.

"Works for me," said Carlie.

"Whatever," said Amy.

"Okay," began Morgan. "For starters, I would like to see us get some kind of new covering for that sorry old couch."

She pointed to the faded and frayed fabric where some of the stuffing was starting to come out. "I mean, we cleaned and scrubbed it the best we could, and that blanket from my house sort of covers it up. But I think we could do better."

"I agree," said Emily.

"Me too," said Carlie.

"How much do you think that will cost?" asked Amy.

Morgan considered this. "I don't know. But we'll get the best deal we can. And while I'm on that subject, I'd like something nicer to cover the bed with too. That mattress is kind of gross and the blanket sort of works, but you know how it slips off. I'd like to do something that makes it prettier and more comfortable. And we need more pillows, you know, so we can lean back there and read and stuff."

Once again, everyone agreed.

"But how much will it cost?" demanded Amy.

"I don't know," Morgan said again. "Do you want to come with me to the fabric store?"

"Why don't we all go?" suggested Carlie.

So it was agreed. After picking up the prize money and dropping off the photos, they would ask Grandma to take them to the fabric store.

"Do you think she'll mind?" asked Emily.

Morgan laughed. "It's a fabric store! She loves those places."

So on Monday they all met at Morgan's house, and Grandma drove them around to do their errands. They made their final stop the fabric store, which happened to be having a big clearance sale. To everyone's relief, they found some great deals on fabric. After several discussions — and near arguments — about color, pattern, and style, they agreed that bright was better and selected a hot pink and orange zebra-striped plush fabric for both the couch and the bed. Amy was the only one with reservations about the bright colors, but even she seemed to be coming around as they picked out some fun prints for pillows.

"I guess I am a little conservative about color," she admitted after everything was laid out in the bus. "I have to admit that this does really perk the place up."

"And just think how good it will feel in here on some gray, foggy day," Morgan pointed out.

"And there are plenty of those," agreed Amy.

Then Morgan put everyone to work on a different part of the sewing project. And by the end of the day, they had both the bed and the couch covered with the new fabric.

"This feels so good," said Amy as the four of them sprawled across the plush-covered bed. "It's like sleeping on a teddy bear."

"Well, I think that was a good accomplishment for today," said Morgan. "We'll work on the pillows tomorrow — maybe even finish up all the sewing completely — and then I have something special planned for Wednesday and Thursday."

"What?" asked Emily.

"An art project," said Morgan. "Something to brighten up the walls."

"How much will it cost?" asked Amy. "You know we only have $48.74 left in our bus fund. And we need to keep some in reserves."

"Reserves?" said Emily.

"Yes. In case of emergencies."

"What kind of emergencies?" asked Carlie.

"You think we might get a flat tire?" teased Morgan.

"Or blow out our engine?" added Emily.

Amy rolled her eyes. "Something could come up. As treasurer, I recommend we keep at least $20 in our reserves. And I think we should consider having monthly fees."

"Is this a business meeting?" asked Morgan, sitting up on the bed and looking at Amy.

"Well, no …"

Morgan flopped back down. "Good."

"But you did say that you like doing things differently," Amy reminded her. "So maybe it's okay to have a business meeting while we're lying down on the bed."

"Fine," said Morgan. "Might as well get it over with. Just so you know, I think keeping some money in our reserves is probably a good idea. And $20 is plenty. But I'm not sure about monthly dues. Although I do think we could come up with ways to earn money if we decided we needed it. I just don't want that to be the main focus of our club." She held up her bracelet. "It's more about friendship, you know."

"I agree," said Emily, relieved that she wouldn't be pressured to come up with ways to pay her monthly dues. As it was, she didn't even have an allowance yet.

"Me too," said Carlie. "Now tell us about the art project, Morgan."

"All I'll say now is that it's going to involve paint." Morgan sighed. "And now for the bad news."

"Bad news?" said Emily, sitting up. The other girls sat up too. Only Morgan remained in a reclined position, a sad expression over her face.

"What bad news?" asked Amy.

"Yeah, out with it," said Carlie. "What's going on?"

"Well, it's funny because I would've considered this good news last summer. In fact, I remember begging my mom for this exact thing."

"What?" demanded Emily as she pulled Morgan up to a sitting position.

"Yeah, quit stringing us along," said Carlie.

"Okay. My mom goes to this big trade show every summer for people who run gift shops or tourist shops or whatever. Anyway, she always comes home with lots of cool free stuff, and it always sounded so fun, and I always used to ask her if I could go. And now she invites me."

"What's so bad about that?" asked Emily.

"I'll be gone for most of a week," said Morgan sadly. "And we've been having so much fun hanging together, and the clubhouse is almost all fixed up, and ..." She flopped back down again. "I'll miss out on all the fun."

"When do you go?" asked Emily.

"Next week." Morgan groaned. "Mom gave me my airline ticket as an early birthday present. There's no backing out now."

"When's your birthday?" asked Amy.

"July 13."

"Oh."

"So you'll be thirteen on the thirteenth?" said Amy.

"Yeah, I guess so."

"Where's the trade show?" asked Emily.

"All the way in Atlanta, Georgia." Morgan just shook her head.

"I think it sounds pretty fun," admitted Emily.

"And glamorous," added Carlie.

"And you get free stuff?" said Amy.

Morgan sat up now and smiled. "But I'll miss you guys so much."

"We'll miss you too," said Emily. "But I'll bet you'll have lots of fun."

"Besides," Amy slapped her forehead. "I almost forgot ... I have music camp next week."

"Music camp?" Morgan frowned. "What is that?"

"It's a camp that focuses on music," said Amy. "Like, duh."

"So you go there and play music?" asked Emily.

"Something like that. You'd have to be into music like I am to fully appreciate it."

Morgan laughed. "In other words, a music geek."

"Hey," said Amy.

"Sorry," said Morgan. "You're not a music geek, Amy. I was just kidding."

"Well, it's kind of true," admitted Amy. "I know I'm a geek. Other kids have been telling me that for years now."

"You are not a geek," said Emily.

"You're just a little uptight sometimes," said Carlie.

"Yeah," said Morgan. "You do need to loosen up, Amy." She laughed as she poked Amy in the ribs. "That's probably why God gave you us."

"Yeah," said Carlie as they all started tickling Amy. "To loosen you up." Then Amy was laughing so loudly that she made a hilarious snorting sound. That got them all laughing so hard that they actually had tears coming down their cheeks.

"Stop! Stop!" laughed Amy, even though the tickling had ended several minutes ago. "Or I'm going to burst."

Finally it quieted down.

"So Amy and I will both be gone," said Morgan. "What are you guys going to do without us?"

"Actually," said Carlie. "It's the Fourth of July this weekend, isn't it?"

"Yeah," said Morgan. "Why?"

"I kind of forgot that I promised my mom I'd watch the boys while she and Tia Maria take a bookkeeping class at the community college. And I just remembered that the class was supposed to be the week after the Fourth of July."

Morgan turned to Emily. "So, let me guess. You're probably going somewhere too?"

Emily just shook her head. "Nope. I'll be here."

Morgan nodded. "Well, then you can look after things for us. I'll put you officially in charge of the bus."

Emily forced a smile. "Gee, thanks."

"Speaking of the Fourth of July," said Morgan. "Anybody got plans?"

"I plan to watch the fireworks." Amy rolled her eyes. "Just like always."

"Yeah," said Morgan. "Did you guys know that you can see the fireworks from right here?"

"Yeah, big deal," said Amy. "Everyone in Harbor View drags out their lawn chairs, sits around watching the big show, and then goes to bed."

"Or you can watch it from the beach," suggested Morgan.

"I think that sounds like fun," said Carlie.

"Maybe we should make it even more fun," said Morgan. "We could invite all the neighbors down for a hot dog roast on the beach, have a big campfire, and then watch the fireworks from there."

"That sounds pretty good," said Amy.

"I think it sounds great," agreed Carlie.

"Maybe it could be a potluck," said Morgan. "I'll see if my grandma wants to help organize it."

And suddenly they were all talking about the Fourth of July. Everyone except for Emily. All she could think about was that she had one whole week of being on her own. What would she do?

chapter eight

The girls, along with the other winners of the First Annual Boscoe Bay Resort Sandcastle-Building Contest, made the front page of Tuesday's newspaper.

"Look at this," said Amy as she read the part about how the girls had won " 'despite the mean-spirited sabotage of their artwork.' "

"They called SpongeBob SquarePants *artwork*!" said Amy.

"It *was* artwork," insisted Morgan as she tossed a finished pillow at Amy's head. The girls were working in the Rainbow Bus stuffing and sewing pillows closed.

Amy said, "Listen to this!"

"Are you still reading the paper?" said Morgan. "You're supposed to be sewing, Amy."

"I needed a break." Amy frowned at her. "Now listen to what I just read on page three. '*Vandals Strike Washington Elementary. Late Sunday night, juvenile vandals spray-painted graffiti and profanity on parts of Washington Elementary. Also, some windows were broken. According to school officials, the building was not entered. Estimate of property damage is listed at about $2,500. A minor has been taken into custody for questioning.*

Police say that spray-paint cans found at the scene may link this crime to a similar act of vandalism that occurred at Harbor View Mobile-Home Court a few weeks ago.'"

"Wow, do you think they caught Derrick Smith?" asked Emily.

"It definitely sounds like they caught the person who destroyed all our hard work cleaning up the trailer park this spring," said Morgan.

By Friday, the girls had completely finished redecorating the inside of the Rainbow Bus. Morgan's interior painting project — geometric designs of spots and stripes and plaids — had provided the bus with just the right final touches that it needed. To celebrate, the girls invited their families and Mr. Greeley to an impromptu "bus warming" that evening after dinner. And, of course, everyone was very impressed.

"I wonder why Mr. Greeley didn't come," said Morgan as they cleaned up the paper cups and napkins afterwards. Grandma, Morgan, and Emily had prepared refreshments of punch and cookies.

"Maybe he was busy," said Carlie as she scooped cookie crumbs from the table into the garbage bag.

"Yeah, right," said Emily. "Probably had a hot date."

They laughed.

"Still, I wish he'd come see it," said Morgan. "Don't you think he'd be pleased with all we've done?"

"I don't know," said Emily as she put the leftover punch in the little fridge. "I still have the feeling that he doesn't want anything to do with the bus. Like he gave it to us just to get it off his hands." What she didn't tell them was her suspicion that there could've been some kind of foul play between Mr. Greeley and Dan Watterson. She knew it was probably just her overactive imagination, but she still didn't trust the old man.

"Whatever the reason ..." said Carlie, collapsing onto their plush couch. "Aren't we glad he did?"

Morgan picked up the beaded curtain that her mom had brought the girls as a housewarming gift. "Should we hang this up here?" she said as she held it up near the front door. "To make a good entrance?"

"That looks beautiful," said Emily as she helped her attach the sticky tape to the ceiling.

"Perfect," said Carlie when they finished.

"It's all perfect," said Amy.

"Then let's call it a night," said Morgan.

"I'm glad they caught the vandal," said Emily as Morgan locked the door to the bus. "I've worried that whoever it was, whether it's Derrick or some other crazy person, might hit our bus."

"I had the same thought," admitted Amy.

"Me too," said Morgan. "I actually pray that God will protect our bus."

"That's a good idea," said Emily.

"Yeah," agreed Carlie as she bent down to pinch a dead leaf off the pot of geraniums that she'd set by the bus door. "Maybe we should do some kind of bus blessing. I've been to house blessings before. You know, when someone moves into a new place, they get their friends to come and bless it. Kind of like our bus warming tonight."

"Good idea," said Morgan. "Maybe we should do it right now."

So the four girls stood outside while Morgan led them in a prayer for the bus, asking God to keep it safe and to make it a happy place for them to hang out together. Then she stopped. "Anyone else want to pray?" So Emily thanked God for giving them the bus as well as their friendships, and she asked God to bless their club.

"Anyone else?" asked Morgan.

So now Carlie prayed, mostly repeating what Morgan and Emily had said, but it sounded sincere.

Morgan glanced at Amy. "You want to add anything?"

Amy just shrugged. "I think that was good. Besides I don't really know how to pray."

"Well, you're going to have to learn," said Morgan.

"Yeah," agreed Emily. "It's not hard. It's just talking to God."

On Saturday night, most of the neighbors of Harbor View Mobile-Home Court trekked down to the beach for a hot dog roast, potluck, and fireworks. And when it was all over with, Amy admitted that it was the best Fourth of July in their neighborhood — ever.

And even though Emily had lived there less than two months, she had to agree.

On Sunday, Morgan handed the bus key over to Emily. And by Monday, everyone seemed to have left town.

Of course, Carlie was still around. But Emily knew that Carlie would have her hands full with her two little brothers. And so Emily would be mostly on her own.

On Monday, Emily slowly walked over to the bus. No reason to hurry since no one would be there today — or anytime this week. It was foggy and chilly this morning and Emily wished she'd put on long pants instead of her thin, cotton shorts. But she remembered that Carlie's dad had recently tested out the little heater to make sure that it was safe. She might be lonely, but she didn't have to be cold. As soon as she was inside and had locked the door (Morgan's recommendation for any of the girls who were in the bus alone), she turned on the heater and just walked around. Morgan had been right about the bright colors. They did make the place feel warm and cheerful on a gray day. Even so, Emily knew it would be much warmer and cheerier if her friends were here. Even Amy, who could be cantankerous sometimes, would be an improvement over this solitude.

"Get over it," she said aloud as she walked to the back of the bus, trying to decide what to do. Then she remembered the box of books that was still underneath the bed. With all their recent activities, she had nearly forgotten it. And now would be a good time to sort and place the books up on the empty bookshelf over the bed. Plus the books would make the place look even better — more lived in. So she removed all the pillows and lifted up the mattress. And there, not only was the box of books, but also the record albums and the record player that they hadn't even tried out yet.

"No time like now," she said as she removed all the items and finally closed the bed and replaced the pillows. First, she took the record player up to the front of the bus. She set it on the passenger seat, near an electrical outlet, and plugged it in. Remembering Mr. Garcia's warning about not running too much electricity at once, she turned off the heater before turning on the record player. To her pleased surprise, it worked.

She went back for the apple crate of old vinyl records, placing it on the floor near the dashboard. Then she began to flip through the records, wondering which one to start with. Finally she decided on Elton John. At least she knew who that was. She slipped the big, black vinyl disk out of the cardboard album jacket, carefully placed it on the turntable, and turned it on. There was a switch with three numbers — 78, 45, and 33. She had no idea what they were for, but remembered hearing Morgan calling these records 33s, so she switched it to that. Then she lifted up the arm and set it to rest on the turning record, and suddenly there was quiet music coming out. She turned the volume up and went to the couch to sit and listen. Very nice. She decided that she liked Elton John.

She left the music playing and started to put books on the shelf. Suddenly it occurred to her that this was kind of nice. She had good music, interesting books, and a cool place to hang out. And it was kind of a relief having it quiet in here for a change. Like it gave her time to think. Plus, with no one chattering away or looking over her shoulder, she could really check out the books as she placed them, one by one, on the shelf. She took her time to open the mysteries, read the first few lines, and decide which one she might like to read first. She noticed that Dan Watterson's name was written in some of the books and, once again, she wondered about this guy. Who he was? And what had been his connection to this bus?

As she was getting the books arranged, she pulled out the old high school yearbook again. She flipped around to the pages that had pictures of Dan Watterson. She noticed that he was most often pictured with a girl with long, dark hair.

Finally Emily found the girl's name by a photo of the two of them in formal attire. Stephanie Chetwood. She looked up the girl in the senior section, but found she wasn't there. So she looked in the junior section and, sure enough, there was Stephanie Chetwood. So she had been a year younger than Dan. Emily thought the girl was really pretty — even by today's standards. She had big, dark eyes and straight, dark hair.

Emily looked back through the handwritten notes in the yearbook, hoping to find what Stephanie had said about Dan. And there, tucked two pages from the back was a very tiny note, written in very small handwriting that had faded a bit with time. Emily squinted to read it. "'To Dan, the love of my life, your Steph.'"

"Wow," said Emily as she read it again. "The love of his life." She closed the book and wondered if they might've gotten married. Maybe Dan graduated and went to college. And maybe Steph did too, and then maybe they got married and had kids. Hey, it was possible that they could actually live in town. Right here in Boscoe Bay! What Emily needed was a phone book. And since they'd just gotten their phone last week, she knew just where to find one.

She turned off the record player, locked the bus, and dashed home to check their new phone book. But there was no Dan Watterson listed. In fact, no one by that last name was listed. She closed the book and sighed. There must be some way to find out this guy's whereabouts. She wished she was brave enough to ask Mr. Greeley, but since he hadn't come to their bus-warming party, and no one had seen him at the Fourth of July hot dog roast, she got the feeling that he was lying low and not wishing for company.

Emily wondered about Morgan's grandma. She knew that Grandma had only lived in Harbor View for the last ten years, after she had retired from teaching high school in another town. It seemed unlikely that she would know. Besides, knowing Morgan, she'd probably already asked. Then Emily remembered Mrs. Hardwick and her son who worked at the newspaper. She seemed to know a lot of people. And she was friendly too. Maybe Emily could ask her. But first she put on her jeans and a sweatshirt. Then she tucked an apple and granola bar into her big front pocket for lunch and took off, heading for Mrs. Hardwick's for a quick visit.

"Sorry to disturb you," she said when the older woman came to the door.

"Not at all," said the woman. "You're Emily, right?"

She nodded. "I don't want to take too much of your time, but I'm curious if you've lived here very long."

"In Harbor View Mobile-Home Court?" asked the woman.

"Yes."

"Goodness, it's been ... let's see ... I think about twenty-five years. Or thereabouts."

"Wow, that's a long time," said Emily.

Mrs. Hardwick laughed. "Well, for a young person, I suppose it seems that way. I was about fifty when I moved here from Ridgeport. My husband had just passed and I didn't like living in a big old house by myself."

Emily nodded. "Did you ever know a man named Dan Watterson?"

Mrs. Hardwick frowned. "The name doesn't sound familiar. Did he live here?"

"Maybe."

"Well, I think I've lived in the court longer than anyone — other than Mr. Greeley."

"How long has he been here?" asked Emily, suddenly wishing she'd thought to write out some questions.

"Well, he started up the place. And it was still pretty new when I moved in here. Only about five or six other mobile homes had been set in place at the time. But I think it had been running for a few years by then." She looked carefully at Emily. "Are you girls working on some new kind of project now? Writing up the history of the place?"

"Not exactly," said Emily. "We're just curious."

Mrs. Hardwick smiled. "Well, that's nice. It's refreshing to see some kids taking an interest in something besides their fancy computers and televisions."

Emily smiled. "Thanks. I better go now."

The old woman waved as Emily walked away. She tried not to laugh about the "fancy computer" comment. Emily hadn't had a computer to use for nearly two months now. And they'd only gotten their hand-me-down TV a week ago. And since they didn't even have cable, it wasn't too tempting to turn into a couch potato. Still, Mrs. Hardwick's computer comment gave Emily an idea. And instead of returning to the bus, Emily headed to town. It was about an eight-minute walk from the trailer park, six if you walked fast. She took her time and ate her apple and granola bar along the way.

Emily had seen the public library from the street, but up until now she hadn't been inside. It was a small building with the same musty book smell that all libraries seemed to have. Emily stopped at the front desk and asked the small, white-haired lady about computers.

"We have four set up right over by the window for public use," said the woman.

"Do you have to have a library card?" asked Emily.

"No, anyone can use them, dear. Just read the rules posted there and be courteous to other patrons."

Emily thanked her and said, "As long as I'm here, may I have an application for a library card? I actually do like to read too."

The woman smiled as she handed her a yellow piece of paper. "Then you came to the right place."

So Emily took the application and went over to the computer section where she logged in and then tried several different searches on the name "Daniel Watterson." The first search, with only his name, provided so many references that it would take her a lifetime to read them all, so she decided to narrow it down by trying his name along with "Boscoe Bay News." This resulted in several old sports stories about the Boscoe Bay Cougars and Dan's athletic contributions during his high school career. There were also many references to college scholarships. So she decided to try those. Unfortunately the ones she attempted to trace seemed to have nothing to do with her Dan Watterson. Finally she gave up.

Before leaving, Emily filled out the library card application and took it back to the woman at the front desk. She felt a little bit guilty for using the name Adams, but she knew that it was for her family's own safety. Her dad might trace down their family here if she used her real name.

"Are you new here?" asked the woman as she glanced down over the application.

"Yes. We've only been here a couple of months."

The woman smiled. "Well, a library card can be a good friend when you're new in town."

Emily was about to tell the woman that even though she was new in town, she did have friends — good friends too.

But she decided that might sound rude. Instead she thanked her.

"Did you wish to check out any books today?"

"No. I have a book that I'm about to start. It's a mystery."

The woman nodded. "Oh, I do love a good mystery. And we have lots of them here."

"Then I'll definitely be back," said Emily. She looked up at the clock on the wall behind the woman and was surprised to see that it was already 4:45, and today was a day when Mom and Kyle got home at five. She'd have to hurry to make it home before them. As she jogged home, she realized that her first day without friends around had passed fairly quickly. Now if only the rest of the week would go this fast.

At dinner, Emily asked her mom about Mr. Greeley. "Don't you think he's kind of weird?" she said after mentioning how he never came to anything social.

"I think he's just sad," said Mom.

"I think he's creepy," said Kyle. "Did you see how long the hair growing out of his ears is? Hey, maybe he's a werewolf."

"Kyle!" Mom glared at him.

"Well, he is strange, Mom," pointed out Emily.

"All I know is he was good to us. When we came here, I didn't have enough money for rent," Mom told them. "He assured me it was okay. He said he understood how people have hard times. And he was very understanding."

"He probably thinks you're hot," said Kyle.

"Kyle!" Mom looked really angry now.

"Sorry."

"Well, you kids be nice to him. He's been good to us. I don't know where we would be if he hadn't been willing to rent this place to me. He's a good-hearted man. Even when I gave him our real name — so he could do a credit check — he promised me that he would keep it secret. And I have no reason not to trust him."

Emily wasn't so sure about that, but she figured if Mom trusted him, maybe she should too. Still, she would keep a safe distance for now!

chapter nine

On Tuesday, Emily returned to the bus with a mission: She would do all she could to figure out who Dan Watterson was. And if she came up with nothing, she would put the case to rest. No sense in making herself crazy over some old dude who happened to leave his high school yearbook in somebody's old bus.

She turned on the record player again, this time turning the Elton John album to the other side, and then she went to the back of the bus to finish putting the books on the shelf. But when she got to the bottom of the box, she saw a small, black book that she hadn't noticed before. She pulled it out to discover it was a journal. And it had been written in. There was no name inside of it, but when she compared the handwriting to the books with Dan Watterson's name written in them, it appeared to be the same. A very neat and angular style that looked more like printing than cursive.

Feeling slightly intrusive, but curious, Emily began to read. And she was thankful — not for the first time — that the other girls weren't around. Not that she planned to hide this from them, but she hated the idea of them making fun of this guy. Emily knew what it was like to keep a journal. She'd been doing so for years. But nothing would humiliate her more as a writer than if someone found her personal thoughts and hopes and dreams and made fun of them. That's why she'd always kept her journals well hidden. It still bothered her deeply that they'd left so quickly that night, she had left a few journals behind. She hoped and prayed her dad never found them.

As Emily read, she felt she could relate to Dan Watterson. He too loved words and aspired to be a writer. He had a column in the school paper, and despite having the image of a jock, he'd secretly written poetry. A lot of poetry. Who would've guessed? She also learned that he did get a sports scholarship to Oregon State, but that he dropped out of college before graduating. And the reason he dropped out was because of a girl. She came to this conclusion since the thing he wrote about most in his journal was Stephanie, his high school sweetheart. It seemed that his devotion was as strong as hers, and that she was the love of his life. But for some reason she had disappeared — left his life without a trace. And as a result, he was lost and heartbroken and devoted many poems to her.

Finally, Emily closed the journal. The last dozen entries were spread out over several years, written from all over the country, but they still sounded very unhappy. As soon as she set the book aside she felt horribly guilty, like she had sneaked into someone's private world. And even though she was still curious, and her desire to solve this Dan the man mystery was strong, she knew she must not go back and reread a single sentence. She also knew that it would be wrong for the other girls to read it too. In fact, she was tempted to destroy the journal altogether. But that seemed wrong too.

Eventually, she decided to find a really good hiding place for it — a place on the bus because it belonged with the bus. The other important thing that Emily learned from the journal was that this had indeed been Dan's bus. He'd bought it from a friend named Jim shortly after he dropped out of college. And even though his dad was furious with him, he lived in this bus, drove around the country, and seemed to have no idea what he would do with his life.

Emily walked around the bus, searching for a safe spot to hide the sad journal. After a thorough search she decided to shove it behind a loose board in the little closet near the bedroom. She felt it would be safe there. As far as Dan went, maybe she would never know anything else. Maybe it was none of her business. But this journal was a private thing and she would respect that.

On Wednesday and Thursday, Emily tried to put thoughts of Dan Watterson behind her as she immersed herself in reading mysteries and writing some poetry of her own. But the more time she spent in the bus, the more she felt that Dan was there too … and the more she felt that this mystery was not going to leave her alone until she had resolved it. So she opened up her own journal and began to write down the questions that seemed to be nagging the loudest.

1. Why is Dan's bus parked at Harbor View?
2. Where is Dan now?
3. What is his relationship to Mr. Greeley?
4. What happened to Stephanie?

And that was about it. Not too difficult, really. Emily scratched her head as she stared at these four questions. It seemed the only way she'd find the answers would be to approach Mr. Greeley. And yet that scared the socks off her.

So she paused and asked herself: *How else do people research these things? What do people in the mystery books do?* She'd already tried the computer without success. This reminded her of the sweet, white-haired librarian, and she wondered, *How long had that woman lived in town?* She might be more helpful than a computer. Besides, she told herself as she walked toward town, she'd soon be out of mysteries. She might as well restock her supply. Hopefully that same librarian would be there again.

Sure enough, the white-haired woman was there. And to Emily's surprise, she even seemed to recognize her.

"Ready for a mystery?" asked the woman when Emily paused in front of her big shiny desk.

"Sort of ..." Emily smiled. "Actually, I'm trying to solve a mystery."

"To solve one?" The woman looked curious.

"And I thought maybe you could help me."

"Me?"

"Yes. That is if you've lived in Boscoe Bay for very long. Have you?"

She laughed. "Well, that depends on how you look at it. It doesn't seem that long to me, but I was born and raised here, and I've lived here all my life."

Emily smiled. "So maybe you can help me. I'm trying to find out about someone. You see I have something that belongs to him — actually a few things — that I found in a box. And I think they might be valuable to him because they're memorabilia. You know what I mean?"

She nodded. "Yes. I can understand that. Who is it you're looking for, dear?"

"Daniel Watterson."

The woman nodded with a creased brow as if trying to remember.

"Do you know him?" Emily asked hopefully.

"I did know him."

"You did?" Emily wanted to jump for joy but—remembering this was a library—controlled herself.

"I used to teach English at the high school. Dan was one of my students. A very bright boy. Popular too. And very good at sports. So much potential ..." Her face grew sad.

"Do you know where he is?" asked Emily. "Does he live around here?"

"Dan died in the Middle East."

"Huh?" Emily frowned at her. "In the Iraq War?"

"No, dear, it was Desert Storm."

"Desert Storm?"

"Do they teach about that in history yet?"

"Not exactly."

"Well, that war was in 1991 and didn't last long. I believe Dan was several years out of college when he went over. I remember being surprised that he'd joined up." She sighed. "And he was one of the unfortunate few who never came back."

"Oh," Emily didn't know what to say, but she could feel tears gathering in her eyes. "Do you mean he was killed?"

She nodded. "I'm sorry to tell you such sad news, dear."

"It's okay." Emily attempted a smile. "I mean it's not your fault. I just had no idea."

"Will you be okay, dear?"

Emily nodded, swallowing against the lump in her throat.

"I don't know what to tell you about the box of memorabilia. The Wattersons left town many years ago, not long after Dan graduated from high school, as I recall. I have no idea where they moved."

"That's okay," said Emily. All she wanted now was to get out of here. She didn't want people to see her crying. "Thanks, Mrs...."

The woman extended her hand. "Mrs. Drimmel," she said.

"Emily Adams." She blinked back tears.

"You take care now," said Mrs. Drimmel. "And next time you come in, I'll show you some good mysteries."

"Thanks." Emily hurried out, trying to hold back the tears as she walked quickly through town. She didn't know why she was taking this so hard, except that it was as if Dan had become a personal friend this week. It was so shocking, so sad, to hear that he was dead. Finally, worried that she might see someone, or someone might see her, Emily began jogging toward home. But instead of going into her house, she went straight to the Rainbow Bus. Then she went inside and locked the door, and she turned on the record player — turned it up loud and just cried.

Finally, after a few minutes, Emily stopped crying. The music was still playing, the same Elton John album that she'd had on just the other day. But this time, as a certain song came on, she listened carefully to the lyrics. The song was about a man, also named Daniel, who was leaving on a plane. He'd had a lot of pain, and now it was time to say good-bye. Emily cried when it came to the line about how Daniel's eyes had died. And then she kept singing the last line: "must be the clouds in my eyes."

The song ended and she turned off the record player. And then she sat down in the driver's seat of the bus and began to pray. "Dear God," she said with her eyes wide open, looking out over the dunes to where she knew the Harbor was. "I know I never really knew Dan Watterson personally, but it feels like I did. And his story is so sad. So very, very sad. Is there anything I can do to help? Or should I just let this thing go? Should I wave good-bye to Daniel and try to forget about it? Please, dear God, show me what to do. Amen."

Then she noticed someone walking along the beach road. At first she felt scared, imagining that she'd just seen Dan's ghost. But then she realized it was only Mr. Greeley. But as she watched him, slowly walking along with his head hanging low, she felt bad. She realized how wrong it was to be suspicious of him — thinking he'd done something to Dan Watterson when he was completely innocent.

She opened the window on the driver's side and called out. "Mr. Greeley?"

He turned to see who it was, then gave her a small half-hearted wave.

"How's it going?" she yelled out the window.

"All right."

Then, without even questioning herself, she hurried outside and ran over to join him. "You taking a walk?" she asked.

"Yep."

"Can I come too?"

He peered curiously at her. "I reckon."

"Going to the beach?" she asked as they began walking.

"Yep."

"Kind of foggy today," she said, wishing for something better to say.

"Yep."

"And cold too."

"Yep."

"We really like our bus, Mr. Greeley."

He turned and looked at her, almost smiling now. "That's good."

"We fixed it all up inside. You should come see it sometime."

He nodded without saying anything, and they just walked in silence for a couple of minutes. Emily was starting to get worried, wondering what on earth she was doing. Why had she come down to the beach with this old guy who she only recently suspected of murder?

"We found some things while we were fixing the bus up ..." she said as they walked toward the Harbor.

He stopped walking. "What kinds of things?"

She stopped walking too. "Personal things."

He frowned. "I took everything off that bus."

"Well, a bunch of things were stored under the bed."

"Under the bed?" He looked skeptical.

"Yeah. There's this kind of secret storage spot there. We found books and record albums and — "

"You said *personal* things?"

"That's right." She studied his face. "Did you know Dan Watterson, Mr. Greeley?"

He slowly nodded.

"He sounded like a really nice guy," said Emily.

"He was."

"I'm curious as to why he left his bus on your property?" she said in a gentle voice. "Was he a friend of yours?"

He nodded again, this time looking off toward the ocean.

"Well, I feel like he was my friend too," she said suddenly.

"Huh?" He looked at her.

"I feel like I know him now." She looked into Mr. Greeley's faded eyes. "This week the other girls have been gone, and I've been reading his books and listening to his music and even reading his journal … and I feel like I really know him." She sighed. "And then I found out how he died in the war." She felt tears coming again, and she knew she wouldn't be able to stop them. "And I've been so sad. I feel like my friend just died."

He nodded, and she saw tears running down his wrinkled old cheeks too. "Yep," he said. "Me too."

"Do you want to talk about it, Mr. Greeley?" she asked.

He peered down at her, and she could almost see him thinking how she was just a kid and wondering why he should talk to her.

"I've been through some hard things too," she told him.

He nodded. "Yep, I s'pect you have."

And so they continued walking, and Mr. Greeley started to talk. And he talked and talked and talked. And finally, after all her investigating and all her wondering and searching, the whole story of Daniel Watterson unfolded. Finally she understood what had happened.

"Wow," she told him as they turned around to walk back toward the trailer court. "That must've been so hard."

He nodded. "Yep."

"Do you think you'd want to read Dan's journal?"

He seemed to consider this. "I guess I would."

"I hid it in the bus. I just didn't think the other girls should read it. Not that I'm trying to be mean. But I'm a writer and I keep a journal, and some things, well, they're supposed to be private, you know?"

He nodded. "And I'm hoping you will keep some parts of my story private too, Emily. I don't mind if you tell your friends that Dan was my son. And you can even tell them about how stupid I was. But some things about Dan ... well, some things are best left alone."

She nodded. "Don't worry. Your story is safe with me."

"And your family's story is safe with me too."

"So does this make us friends now?" asked Emily as they headed down the dunes trail that led back toward the trailer court.

"I reckon it does."

Emily paused where the trail forked over to the bus. "How about if I get that journal while we're here?"

"I'd like that."

"You want to see the bus?" she asked, waiting and hoping that he'd follow her down the trail. "We've really fixed it up."

So while she got the journal, he took a quick peek inside, but then just as quickly he went back outside. "It sure looks different in there," he said as she came out to rejoin him.

"Kind of girly, huh?"

He grinned. "Yep, I reckon it is. But it does look nice."

Then she gave him the journal as well as the high school yearbook. "Oh, yeah," she said. "Do you have a record player?"

He nodded.

"Let me get something else for you, okay?" And she hurried back in to get the Elton John album. "Listen to the song called 'Daniel' on this record," she told him. "I think you'll like it."

He nodded and started to go, but then he stopped. "And since you feel like Dan was your friend too, well, you'd be welcome to come see some of his photos and other things if you'd like. Your friends can come too. I have them all set up in a room. Just to look at. I thought I'd gotten all of his stuff from the bus." He looked at the items in his hand. "Guess I missed some. Thank you for taking the time, Emily."

"*Thank you*, Mr. Greeley."

chapter ten

"Thanks for letting me come with you today," Emily said as she rode with Morgan's grandma to the airport. It was Saturday afternoon and Morgan and her mom's flight should've landed by now.

"We're supposed to get them by the baggage pickup," said Grandma as she turned toward the terminal. "You keep your eyes peeled and I'll drive as slowly as possible."

"No problem there," said Emily when she noticed the traffic jam up ahead. Grandma slowly made her way forward and Emily scanned the crowd for Morgan and her mom. "There they are!" she shouted. "Up there by the big turning door."

Soon they had Morgan and her mom and their stuff all loaded in the car and were heading out. "Thanks for the ride, Mom," said Cleo. "But I thought Leslie was getting us."

"She had to keep shop for you," said Grandma, "since Kara was sick today."

"I'm so glad you came!" said Morgan as she gave Emily's hand a squeeze. "I missed you so much. So tell me, have you been bored out of your gourd?"

"Not exactly," said Emily with a smile. "Although I'll admit that it has been pretty quiet."

"Have you seen Carlie at all?"

"A couple of times … but she's been pretty busy with Miguel and Pedro. They're a handful. But I did help her take them to the beach yesterday. The weather finally warmed up again, and we played in the sand and stuff."

"I'm so happy to be home," said Morgan. "I mean, it was actually pretty fun in Atlanta. And I can't wait to show you guys some of the awesome stuff I got for free at the gift show — things we can use for the bus. Very cool."

"I'm so glad you're home too," admitted Emily. Then she lowered her voice, "and I do have something *big* to tell you when we're all together, back in our clubhouse again."

"Can't you tell me now?" begged Morgan. "It sounds really interesting."

Emily shook her head. "Remember what you said about being part of a club, Morgan. We need to consider the other girls too." Then she held up her hand with the bracelet and grinned. "Rainbows rule."

Morgan nodded and held hers up too. "Rainbows rule."

By the time they made it home from Portland, it was too late to have a club meeting, but Morgan said she'd call the girls for a two o'clock meeting tomorrow, after they got back from church.

"Sure you don't want to give me a hint about your big news?" asked Morgan as they dropped Emily at her house.

"It's a mystery," said Emily.

"Thanks a lot," said Morgan. But she was smiling.

"Glad you're home," said Emily again. "See you tomorrow."

The next day, on their way home from church, Morgan tried to pry more information from Emily, but Emily told her she'd have to wait.

"You're pretty good at keeping a secret," said Morgan as they pulled into the mobile-home court.

Emily nodded with lips pressed firmly together. Morgan had no idea!

Finally it was two o'clock and all four girls were back together in the Rainbow Bus. Emily put on a record to play, and they sat down at the table where Morgan set out a plate of her grandma's homemade oatmeal raisin cookies and a carton of milk. She'd also brought along a box full of things from the gift show for the bus. She had colorful notepads and magnetic pens and scented candles and bright silk flowers and stuffed gadgets and window decorations and all sorts of things.

"You should've seen the place," said Morgan. "It was huge, like acres and acres of these little shops with all this stuff. My feet got so tired."

"But was it fun?" asked Amy.

"Sure. And then they give you all this free stuff."

"It's like Christmas," said Carlie, holding up a stained-glass butterfly with a little hanger on it.

"For the bus," added Morgan. "Which reminds me, I did get some Christmas decorations too, but we can save those for later."

"It's so good to be back in the bus," said Amy. "And it's fun having music. That's a great place for the record player."

"So, how was music camp?" asked Emily, wanting to save her news for last.

Amy gave a complete rundown on music camp and who was there and how Amy got to do a flute solo at the campfire one night. "It was really pretty good," she said finally. "And it didn't seem that geeky."

"See," said Morgan. "We told you."

"And I made $100 this week," said Carlie proudly.

"Just for babysitting?" asked Amy.

"Just for?" repeated Carlie with wide eyes. "Do you have any idea how much work it is to take care of two little kids that never stop moving? And Pedro is barely potty trained. You know what that means?"

Amy laughed. "No. But it doesn't sound good."

"Well, that was a hard-earned $100," said Carlie. "And then my parents made me put half into the bank for my college fund. And the rest ... Mom says I should save to buy school clothes." She shook her head. "I think they're the ones who came out on top in that deal."

The bus got quiet now, and Morgan looked at Emily. "Emily has something to tell us," she said. "Something big."

Now all eyes were on Emily. Thankfully, she'd carefully rehearsed what she was going to tell them — and how much. She wanted to be respectful of Mr. Greeley, but she wanted them to understand the story too. Especially since they all got to share in the bus together.

"Well, I was putting away the books and I started wondering about Dan Watterson again."

"Oh, yeah, Dan the man," said Amy. "We almost forgot about that dude."

"That's right," said Morgan. "Don't tell me you figured it out?"

Emily nodded. "And it wasn't easy." She told them about some of her early dead ends and then how she finally remembered the old librarian. But she didn't mention the journal. She wanted that to remain private.

"Mrs. Drimmel?" said Amy. "Of course, she's been here forever."

"And she's so old, she'd know everybody," said Morgan. "Good work, Em."

"She was Dan's teacher in high school," said Emily. "And she totally remembered him. She said he was a nice kid. But she also said that shortly after college he went to Desert Storm."

"Desert Storm?" said Carlie. "What's that?"

"A war," said Emily.

"The Iraq War?" asked Amy.

"No, that's what I thought too. Desert Storm started in 1991, and Dan went in that year."

"He would've been about twenty-eight by then," said Amy.

"Thirty," corrected Emily, and everyone looked stunned. "I guess he had a late birthday," she added quickly. "Anyway, Dan Watterson was killed in action."

"Really?" Morgan looked stunned.

"That's sad," said Carlie.

"War is so wrong," said Amy in an angry voice.

"So he never made it back," continued Emily. "And this was his bus. He'd been touring the country in it ... after college. And he was kind of lost and confused ... He'd been in love with this girl from high school, and she sort of just disappeared on him. It was like he never got over her."

"Man, that's so sad," said Morgan.

"Was that why he went to the war?" asked Carlie.

"Maybe so ..."

"But why is his bus here?" asked Morgan.

"Well, that's the amazing part," said Emily. "Dan Watterson was Mr. Greeley's only son."

"But why wasn't his name Greeley?" asked Morgan.

"Mr. Greeley's wife left him when Dan was a little boy. She married another man who adopted Dan, and they changed his name. And poor Mr. Greeley didn't see Dan for years. He finally tracked them down in Boscoe Bay and moved here himself. That's when he started the mobile-home court. Dan was still in high school. He just wanted to be around him."

"That's sweet," said Morgan.

"Yeah. And they got to be friends and stuff."

"And then Dan went to the war and got killed?" said Carlie, her voice breaking as she said it.

Emily nodded. "Yeah. I was really torn up about it too. I felt like I'd really gotten to know Dan, like we were related or something."

"Well, we'll have to make sure that we honor his memory in our bus," said Morgan. "Maybe we can hang up a picture or something."

"That's a great idea," said Emily. "I'll talk to Mr. Greeley about it."

Morgan peered curiously at her. "So you're talking to Mr. Greeley now?"

Emily grinned. "Yeah. He's really nice. Just sad and lonely. But we're friends now. And he told me it was okay to tell you guys about Dan's story — since we're the owners of his bus."

"That's cool," said Morgan.

"So what kind of Christmas stuff did you get at the gift show?" asked Emily, quickly changing the subject.

"Huh?" said Morgan, caught off guard.

"Like, did you get any cool strings of lights?" asked Emily hopefully. "I was thinking that it'd be cool to hang some string lights in here. You know for those gray, foggy kinds of days, like the ones we had last week."

"That's a great idea," said Morgan. "And I did get a set of lights. They were actually the shapes of tropical fruit."

"That's perfect!" exclaimed Emily.

"You want to see them?"

"Yeah!" said Emily.

"Okay." Morgan was already pushing through the beads and going for the door. "I'll be back in five minutes."

As soon as Morgan was gone, Emily started talking. "Okay, you guys, it's Morgan's birthday on Tuesday, and I wanted to get her out of here so we could make a quick plan. All in favor of giving her a surprise birthday party say aye."

"Aye!" all three shouted.

"Okay." Emily grabbed the notebook. "Who's doing what?"

It was the quickest party-planning meeting Emily had ever been to, not that she'd been to many. But by the time Morgan came back, they had it all figured out. And to make their little act even more convincing, Emily got very excited over Morgan's tropical-fruit lights.

"Those are so great, Morgan!" she exclaimed as Morgan took them out of the box.

"They'll be perfect in here," said Amy.

"And I bet they don't use much electricity either," added Carlie.

"Good thinking to bring them in here, Em," said Morgan. "I'm really glad I didn't save them until Christmas."

"Well, I was in here a lot last week," said Emily. "And it was pretty gloomy outside. Seemed like we could use some more light."

Soon they had the lights suspended over the tiny dining table, and when Morgan plugged them in, everyone cheered.

"Look at all the colors," said Emily.

"Sort of like a rainbow," said Amy.

"Rainbows rule!" shouted Carlie, holding up her hand with the bracelet. And the other girls followed.

"It's good to be back together again," Morgan said with a big smile.

They spent the next couple of hours just hanging out, putting all Morgan's interesting goodies away, and listening to old vinyl records. And Emily thought it felt almost like coming home.

On Monday, Emily left the trailer park just a little before nine. She used the back exit so that Morgan wouldn't notice her from her kitchen window. Then she hurried toward town and finally turned into the Waterfront District where she knew Morgan's mom's shop was located. She'd seen Cleo's from the street, but up until now had never gone inside. But today she was on a mission.

"Oh, hi, Emily," said Cleo from where she was unpacking a box in the back of the store.

"Hi," said Emily, looking around the shop with interest, noticing all the colorful items from all over the world. There were pillows and dishes and statues and jewelry and clothing — all sorts of things. "This is a cool shop," she told Cleo as she walked toward the back.

"You've never been in here before?" asked Cleo as she unwrapped a large piece of pottery and set it on the counter.

"No, but I'll be sure to make it a regular stop from now on."

"So, what's up?" asked Cleo as she adjusted a brightly colored scarf that was tied loosely around her neck.

"I'm looking for something for Morgan's birthday," said Emily.

"That's so sweet of you," said Cleo.

"We're having a surprise party for her tomorrow — in the clubhouse — and I wanted to give her something special." Emily reached down to pat the small purse that was hanging over her shoulder. She still had most of her share of the people's choice winnings, but she'd need to save enough to buy birthday cake ingredients too. "Do you know of anything she's been wanting?"

Cleo rubbed her chin as she considered this. "Hmm ..." Then she snapped her fingers. "I do!"

"What is it?"

"Come over here and I'll show you."

Emily hoped it wouldn't be too expensive as she followed Cleo over to where some wooden boxes were stacked. They looked really nice. Then Cleo picked up one of the larger ones and opened it. "Morgan's been wanting something just like this to keep her beadwork in."

"It's beautiful," said Emily, running her hand over the smooth surface of the wood. "How much does it cost?"

"Well," said Cleo, "how about if I give it to you at cost?"

Emily wasn't sure what that meant, but she nodded.

"That would be ten dollars."

"Really?" Emily couldn't believe it. How could a box this nice be that inexpensive? "Are you sure?" she asked. "I mean, I don't want you to — "

"I'm sure, Emily. You see, all my things are imported and I get some amazing buys. And, as I recall, cost on these boxes was really about ten dollars."

"Well, I'll take it," said Emily.

Cleo smiled. "Want me to wrap it for you?"

"Oh, yeah," said Emily. "I don't think we have any wrapping paper at home."

"Go ahead and look around the shop," said Cleo as she carried the box back to the counter.

Before long, the gift was wrapped and paid for and Emily was happily carrying the brown bag through town. She stopped by the little grocery store to get the cake things, including birthday candles, then headed on home.

"Watcha doing?" asked Morgan as Emily came into Harbor View with her bag.

"Just some shopping," said Emily, wishing she'd remembered to use the other entrance. "For my mom," she added, feeling a little guilty for the lie. But maybe it was okay under the circumstances.

The four girls got together to hang out in the afternoon, but no mention was made of the upcoming birthday, and Emily suspected that Morgan was feeling a little bummed that no one seemed to remember her big day. Then everyone, except Morgan, made up excuses to go home early. Emily knew it was so they could take care of their parts of the party preparations. Carlie was in charge of decorations, and she was going to make a mini-pinata. Amy was taking care of napkins and plates and things, promising that it would be really pretty.

"You guys coming over tomorrow?" asked Morgan as they went outside.

"I can't come over until one," said Carlie. "I have to babysit."

"And I promised to help at the restaurant tomorrow morning," said Amy.

"Why don't we just get together at one then?" suggested Emily, knowing full well that the three girls would be there sooner. And she'd already arranged with Morgan's grandma to sneak the bus key out and into the mailbox while Morgan was still asleep.

"Okay," said Morgan. But she looked disappointed.

"See ya tomorrow," called Emily as she left Morgan still standing by the abandoned bus.

The next day, Emily, Carlie, and Amy sneaked over to the bus at noon. Carlie had gotten the key out of the mailbox, and they let themselves in and quickly went to work setting up their surprise party. Shortly before one, the three girls stepped back to look at their accomplishment.

"The decorations are fantastic, Carlie," said Emily.

"Yes," agreed Amy. "So colorful. Morgan will love it."

"And the dishes and things you brought . . . ," said Emily. "They're perfect too, Amy."

"That cake looks yummy," said Carlie.

"It's almost one," said Emily. "We should hide in the back of the bus."

"What if Morgan doesn't come?" asked Amy. "She might be worried about the lost key."

"I think she'll come," said Emily. "She'll have to explain to us why we can't get in the bus."

"But we won't be here," said Carlie. "If we're hiding."

"I'll leave the door open," said Emily. She ran up to open the door then back to where Amy and Carlie were waiting.

After about five minutes, they heard someone coming in the door. And sure enough it was Morgan. They all jumped out and yelled, "Surprise!"

"Whoa!" said Morgan, almost falling backwards out the door.

"Happy Birthday!" they yelled.

It was obvious that she was totally surprised, and this made the three girls even happier.

"You're a teenager now!" said Emily, giving Morgan a quick hug.

Morgan grinned. "And you guys aren't."

"I will be in November," said Emily.

"I won't be thirteen until next April," said Carlie.

"And I won't be thirteen for almost two years," admitted Amy. "How come you're so old anyway, Morgan?"

Morgan laughed. "My mom and I were living in Thailand when I was six, and she didn't start me in school."

"So you weren't held back?" said Amy.

"Amy!" said Emily in a scolding tone.

But Morgan just laughed even harder now. "No, Amy, I wasn't held back. I just didn't start first grade until I was seven. But I never really minded. I actually think it's pretty cool being older than everyone."

"I think it's cool that you got to live in Thailand," said Emily. "You'll have to tell us more about that."

"Not right now," said Morgan, eyeing the cake and presents.

And so Emily lit the thirteen rainbow-colored candles, they sang "Happy Birthday," and then Morgan blew them all out in one big breath.

"You'll get your wish!" exclaimed Emily.

"I already did," said Morgan, smiling at her three best friends. "It seems like my prayers and wishes just keep coming true."

chapter one

"I can't hang with you guys today." Carlie kicked a rock with the toe of her sandal and frowned.

"Why not?" asked Morgan as she unlocked the door to the Rainbow Bus, the girls' clubhouse. "Did you forget that I was going to teach you how to do beads today?"

"No." Carlie rolled her eyes. "But Tia Maria is making me go to work with her today."

"Huh?" Emily peered curiously at Carlie. "Don't they have child labor laws in this state?"

"Yeah," said Amy. "First they make you babysit all the time and now they have you cleaning houses too? What's up with that?"

"I don't babysit *all the time*," Carlie corrected her. "Besides, I sometimes get paid for it when I do."

"Why do you have to go and help your aunt with house-cleaning today?" asked Morgan.

"That's not what I'll be doing," Carlie explained. "I'm going with Tia Maria because she's working for this new family that moved to town last week. They have a girl who's the same grade as us, and she's all bummed about having to move here and not knowing anyone. And it doesn't help that school starts in a couple of weeks."

"So they're going to force you to become her friend?" questioned Amy. "Isn't that a little weird?"

Carlie nodded. "Yep. And that's exactly what I told Tia Maria too, but she won't take no for an answer. She's certain that I'm going to like this new girl."

"What if you don't?" asked Morgan.

Carlie shrugged. "Nothing I can do about that. But I got to thinking ... I mean, I remember how it felt to be new in town last spring ... and maybe I should try to make her feel welcome. Her name's Chelsea Landers. And, who knows, maybe she's nice."

"Well, if she is nice, maybe we should all get to know her," suggested Morgan. "Maybe she'll even want to join our club."

"I don't know," said Amy. "I mean, we've never talked about getting new members before. Do you guys really think it's a good idea?"

"I'm not so sure," admitted Emily. "The bus isn't really that big. With all four of us it can get kinda crowded."

"Well, there'll only be three of us today," Morgan pointed out. "Sorry you can't stay." Morgan smiled at Carlie. "But maybe I can show you how to do beads some other time."

"Yeah," said Carlie. "I hope so."

"Well, have fun," called Emily.

Carlie tried to hide her disappointment as she waved. "See ya guys later."

The other girls called out good-bye and Carlie slowly walked back toward her house. This really didn't seem fair. She'd already missed out on a lot of fun this summer because of babysitting her little brothers so much. Plus, she'd been looking forward to learning how to do beads for weeks now. But she had to go be a "play date" for someone she didn't even know. She was tempted to tell Tia Maria to forget it, but Tia Maria was her favorite aunt and really cared about Carlie. So maybe she should just bite the bullet, put a smile on her face, and go.

"Hey, Carlie," called Tia Maria. She was standing by her little red car and waving. "I've been waiting for you."

"I'm coming," said Carlie. "I just had to tell my friends that I wouldn't be around today."

"I hope you don't mind too much," said Tia Maria.

Carlie shrugged as she got into the car. "It's okay. I mean, I do remember how lonely I felt when we first moved here."

"And then you made friends with the girls from the trailer court," Tia Maria reminded her. "And you've been happy as a clam ever since."

Carlie forced a smile. "Yeah, it's great having good friends." But she thought it would be even better if she actually got to hang with them sometimes!

"Especially when you are in middle school," Tia Maria pointed out. "I still remember how hard it was going to seventh grade. My best friend had moved away that summer and I felt like I didn't know a soul. I was so scared."

"Do you think that's how Chelsea feels?" asked Carlie.

Tia Maria nodded. "Yeah. She's a gloomy girl."

Carlie sat up straighter now. "Well, I'll do my best to try and cheer her up. I just hope she's nice." The truth was, ever since moving to Boscoe Bay last spring, Carlie had been wishing for a best friend for herself. It seemed like Emily and Morgan had become best friends during the summer, and even though there was still Amy ... well, Carlie just wasn't too sure. She and Amy were so completely different.

"Speaking of nice," said Tia Maria. "You look very pretty today."

Available now at your local bookstore!

visit faiThGirLz.com
inner beauty, outward faith

Project: Rescue Chelsea

Book Three • Softcover • ISBN 0-310-71188-6

Carlie makes a new friend. Chelsea Landers lives in a mansion and isn't always very kind. Carlie would like a best friend, but will Chelsea fit in with her other friends? When Carlie is betrayed by Chelsea, she learns how much she appreciates her friends in the Rainbow Club. This is a story about forgiveness and accepting differences

Project: Take Charge

Book Four • Softcover • ISBN 0-310-71189-4

The girls of 622 Harbor View find out their town's only city park has been vandalized and may soon be turned into a parking lot. They group together to save their beloved park and soon meet an elderly woman with the power to help their cause, or stop it before it even starts. But will they be able to convince her to help before it's too late?

visit faiThGirLz.com

inner beauty, outward faith

Faithgirlz! is based on 2 Corinthians 4:18—So we fix our eyes not on what is seen, but on what is unseen. For what is seen is temporary, but what is unseen is eternal (NIV)—and helps girls find Inner Beauty, Outward Faith.